SH

*An Anthology of
Canadian Ghost Stories*

Edited by

Greg Ioannou
and
Lynne Missen

SEAL BOOKS
McClelland-Bantam, Inc.
Toronto

A SEAL BOOK/MAY 1990

ISBN 0-7704-2349-3

PRINTED IN CANADA

0 9 8 7 6 5 4 3 2 1

COPYRIGHT NOTICES AND ACKNOWLEDGEMENTS

Contents

Introduction   Greg Ioannou   vi

House Party at Smoky Island   *L. M. Montgomery*   1

August   *Garfield Reeves-Stevens*   14

Coffins for Two   *Vincent Starrett*   21

The Money Box   *Elaine Driedger*   29

The Charlottetown Banquet   *Robertson Davies* ..   40

The Prophetess   *Francis Owen*   53

Under the Elms   *Gail Herbert*   64

The Angel   *Robin Skelton*   84

O.R.3   *Karen Wehrstein*   90

The Country Doctor   *Marian Engel*   113

CHIPS   *Judith and Garfield Reeves-Stevens*   133

The Perdu   *Sir Charles G. D. Roberts*   151

About Effie   *Timothy Findley*   168

The Fighting Spirit   *Rudy Kremberg*   183

Lavender Lady   *Karen Voss Peters*   193

The Ghost of Firozsha Baag   *Rohinton Mistry* ...   198

Introduction

The phone rang. It was Seal Books.

"We're considering publishing an anthology of ghost stories written by Canadians. Interested in putting it together for us?" I sat down with my assistant, Lynne Missen, who had been editing an accounting textbook. "Fiction? I'm going to work on some fiction? But you *always* hog whatever fiction comes in." I ignored her.

We drew up a list of every Canadian writer we could remember ever having written anything ghosty. Robertson Davies. Robin Skelton. Hmmm. Davies, Skelton . . . there must be others.

We decided on a division of labour: I would phone around and scare up some previously unpublished stories; Lynne would bury herself in the Metro Toronto Reference Library, finding as many ghost stories as she could. This is work?

We started with one of Davies' annual Massey College stories. (Lynne wanted to use the one about the graduate student who had failed his examination. I preferred the one about the Charlottetown Banquet, having an inclination towards anything to do with food. If there is ever a *Let's Shiver Again*, the graduate student story will grace it.)

Lynne quickly turned up all sorts of amazing things for us to choose from. Some of the ones we selected are from well-known writers: Timothy Findley, Marian Engel, Lucy Maud Montgomery. Others are less well known: Francis Owen, Vincent Starrett, Rohinton Mistry (who won't remain obscure for long!), and Charles G. D. Roberts. Yet we discovered that it was a little more difficult finding Canadian ghost stories than we had planned—particularly stories that haven't been included in loads of other anthologies.

The collections of ghost stories Lynne looked at were more often than not by American or British writers. Many of the stories she did find were verging on the supernatural, rather than being ghostly, so the focus of the book shifted slightly to include some arguable ghosts.

While looking for stories, we confronted some fairly basic literary questions, beyond the basic what is the difference between a ghost, a spirit, a doppelgänger, a shade, a phantom, a phantasm, a wraith . . . ? (The intricate answers are far too long to go into here.) Why is there such a wealth of short stories by Canadians? (Probably because for decades magazines — literary and otherwise — provided a ready market for Canadian writers by publishing their short stories.) Why do writers from all countries, from virtually all cultures, write thematically similar ghost stories? (A question for anthropologists and comparative religion majors, not for editors.)

I left Lynne burrowed in the library, trying to decide what exactly constitutes a ghost, while I contacted some writer friends. Several of them quickly sent me their ghost stories. The first three originals (from Elaine Driedger, Gail Herbert, and Rudy Kremberg) came in at about the same time, and all were good enough to have me eagerly seeking out more.

Soon after, original ghost stories seemed to turn up out of nowhere. Gar Reeves-Stevens was delighted, he said, to send me a story he'd been thinking about for a while — and was I interested in one his wife, Judy, was writing with him? And would I like to come to a party to launch his new novel? (Would *I* like to go to a party?) At the party, I chatted with Karen Wehrstein (who was thinking about writing a ghost story). The next day, I was talking to Karen Voss Peters about the novel she is working on, and she started talking about short stories . . .

We hope you enjoy what we have come up with. We think the collection is varied enough that everyone will find lots to their liking. Some of the stories will make you smile, others will make you shiver. Although some of the stories are by internationally known writers, many are by people who are just starting to make reputations for themselves. We know you'll be as excited by their talent as we are.

Greg Ioannou
Toronto
January, 1990

House Party at Smoky Island

L. M. Montgomery

Lucy Maud Montgomery is so strongly associated with *Anne of Green Gables* and its infinite series of sequels that it is forgotten that she was also a prominent poet and diarist, and a prolific short story writer, with approximately five hundred stories published.

This one first appeared in the wonderful American pulp fiction magazine *Weird Tales*, which from 1923 to 1954 fostered such writers as H. P. Lovecraft and Ray Bradbury. *Weird Tales* saw the birth of Conan the Barbarian and the whole swords and sorcery genre, and for three decades was virtually the only magazine that would carry horror stories—and ghost stories.

Try to imagine this story in context, perhaps sandwiched between the newest Conan episode and some wildly inventive C. L. Moore story set on Mars. A long, long way from Anne's home on Prince Edward Island.

When Madeline Stanwyck asked me to join her house party at Smoky Island I was not at first disposed to do so. It was too early in the season, and there would be mosquitoes. One mosquito can keep me more awake than a bad conscience and there are millions of mosquitoes in Muskoka.

"No, no, the season for them is over," Madeline assured me. Madeline would say anything to get her way.

"The mosquito season is never over in Muskoka," I said, as grumpily as anyone could speak to Madeline. "They thrive up there at zero. And even if by some miracle there are no mosquitoes, I've no hankering to be chewed to pieces by black flies.''

Even Madeline did not dare to say there would be no black flies, so she wisely fell back on her Madelinity.

''Please come, for my sake,'' she said wistfully. ''It wouldn't be a real party for me if you weren't there, Jim darling.''

I am Madeline's favourite cousin, twenty years her senior, and she calls everybody darling when she wants to get something out of him. Not but that Madeline . . . but this story is not about Madeline. It is about an occurence which took place at Smoky Island. None of us pretends to understand it, except the judge, who pretends to understand everything. But he really understands it no better than the rest of us. His latest explanation is that we were all hypnotized and in the state of hypnosis saw and remembered things we couldn't otherwise have seen or remembered. But even he cannot explain who or what hypnotized us.

I decided to yield, but not all at once. ''Has your Smoky Island housekeeper still got that detestable white parrot?'' I asked.

''Yes, but it is much better mannered than it used to be,'' assured Madeline. ''And you know you have always liked her cat.''

''Who'll be in your party? I'm rather finicky as to the company I keep.''

Madeline grinned. ''You know I never invite anyone but interesting people to my parties'' — I bowed to the implied compliment — ''with a dull one or two to show off the sparkle of the rest of us''—I did not bow this time — ''Consuelo Anderson . . . Aunt Alma . . . Professor Tennant and his wife . . . Dick Lane . . . Tod Newman

. . . Old Nosey . . . Min Ingrams . . . Judge Walden . . . Mary Harland . . . and a few Bright Young Things to amuse *me*."

I ran over the list in my mind, not disapprovingly. Consuelo was a very fat girl with a B.A. degree. I liked her because she could sit still for a longer time than any other woman I know. Tennant was professor of something he called New Pathology — an insignificant little man with a gigantic intellect. Dick Lane was one of those coming men who never seem to arrive, but a frank, friendly, charming fellow enough. Mary Harland was a comfortable spinster, Tod an amusing little fop. Aunt Alma a sweet, silvery-haired thing like a Whistler mother. Old Nosey — whose real name was Miss Alexander and who never let anyone forget that she had nearly sailed on the *Lusitania* — and the Malcolms who had no terrors for me, although the Senator always called his wife Kittens. And Judge Walden was an old crony of mine. I did not like Min Ingram, who had a rapier-like tongue, but she could be ignored, along with the Bright Young Things.

"Is that all?" I asked cautiously.

"Well . . . Dr. Armstrong and Brenda, of course," said Madeline, eyeing me as if it were not at all of course.

"Is that—wise?" I said slowly.

Madeline crumpled. "Of course not," she said miserably. "It would likely spoil everything. But John insists on it . . . you know he and Anthony Armstrong have been pals all their lives. And Brenda and I have always been chummy. It would look so funny if we didn't have them. I don't know what has got into her. We all *know* Anthony never poisoned Susette."

"Brenda doesn't know it, apparently," I said.

"Well, she ought to!" snapped Madeline. "As if Anthony could have poisoned anyone! But that's one of the reasons I particularly wanted you to come."

"Ah, now we're getting at it. But why *me*?"

"Because you've more influence over Brenda than anyone else . . . oh yes, you have. If you could get her to open up . . . talk to her . . . you might help her. Because . . . if something doesn't help her soon she'll be beyond help. You know that."

I knew it well enough. The case of the Anthony Armstrongs was worrying us all. We saw a tragedy being enacted before our eyes and we could not lift a finger to help. For Brenda would not talk and Anthony had never talked.

The story, now five years old, was known to all of us, of course. Anthony's first wife had been Susette Wilder. Of the dead nothing but good; so I will say of Susette only that she was very beautiful and very rich. Luckily her fortune had come to her unexpectedly by the death of an aunt and cousin after she had married Anthony, so that he could not be accused of fortune-hunting. He had been wildly in love with Susette at first, but after they had been married a few years I don't think he had much affection left for her. None of the rest of us had ever had any to begin with. When word came back from California — where Anthony had taken her one winter for her nerves — that she was dead I don't suppose anyone felt any regret, nor any suspicion when we heard that she had died from an overdose of chloral; rather mysteriously, to be sure, for Susette was neither careless nor suicidally inclined. There were some ugly rumours, especially when it became known that Anthony had inherited her entire fortune under her will; but nobody ever dared say much openly. We, who knew and loved Anthony, never paid any heed to the hints. And when, two years later, he married Brenda Young, we were all glad. Anthony, we said, would have some real happiness now.

For a time he did have it. Nobody could doubt that he and Brenda were ecstatically happy. Brenda was a sincere, spiritual creature, lovely after a fashion totally different from Susette. Susette had had gold hair and eyes as cool and green as fluorspar. Brenda had slim, dark distinction, hair that blended with the dusk, and eyes so full of twilight that it was hard to say whether they were blue or grey. She loved Anthony so terribly that sometimes I thought she was tempting the gods.

Then—slowly, subtly, remorselessly—the change set in. We began to feel that there was something wrong— very wrong—between the Armstrongs. They were no longer quite so happy . . . they were not happy at all . . . they were wretched. Brenda's old delightful laugh was never heard, and Anthony went about his work with an air of abstraction that didn't please his patients. His practice had fallen off awhile before Susette's death, but it had picked up and grown wonderfully. Now it began dropping again. And the worst of it was that Anthony didn't seem to care. Of course he didn't need it from a financial point of view, but he had always been so keenly interested in his work.

I don't know whether it was merely surmise or whether Brenda had let a word slip, but we all knew or felt that a horrible suspicion possessed her. There was some whisper of an anonymous letter, full of vile innuendoes, that had started the trouble. I never knew the rights of that, but I did know that Brenda had become a haunted woman.

Had Anthony given Susette that overdose of chloral—given it purposely?

If she had been the kind of woman who talks things out, some of us might have saved her. But she wasn't. It's my belief that she never said one word to Anthony about the cold horror of distrust that was poisoning her life. But he must have felt she suspected him, and between them was the chill and shadow of a thing that must not be spoken of.

At the time of Madeline's house party the state of affairs between the Armstrongs was such that Brenda had almost reached the breaking-point. Anthony's nerves were tense, too, and his eyes were almost as tragic as hers. We were all ready to hear that Brenda had left him or done something more desperate still. And nobody could do a thing to help, not even I, in spite of Madeline's foolish hopes. I couldn't go to Brenda and say, "Look here, you know, Anthony never thought of such a thing as poisoning Susette." After all, in spite of our surmises, the trouble might be something else altogether. And if she did suspect him, what proof could I offer her that would root the obsession out of her mind?

I hardly thought the Armstrongs would go to Smoky Island, but they did. When Anthony turned on the wharf and held out his hand to assist Brenda from the motorboat, she ignored it, stepping swiftly off without any assistance and running up through the rock garden and the pointed firs. I saw Anthony go very white. I felt a little sick myself. If matters had come to such a pass that she shrank from his mere touch, disaster was near.

Smoky Island was in a little blue Muskoka lake and the house was called the Wigwam . . . probably because nothing on Earth could be less like a wigwam. The Stanwyck money had made a wonderful place of it, but even the Stanwyck money could not buy fine weather. Madeline's party was a flop. It rained every day more or less for the week, and though we all tried heroically to make the best of things, I don't think I ever spent a more unpleasant time. The parrot's manners were no better, in spite of Madeline's assurances. Min Ingram had brought along an aloof, disdainful dog with her that everyone hated because he despised us all. Min herself kept passing out needle-like insults when she saw anyone in danger of being comfortable. I thought the Bright Young Things seemed to hold *me* responsible for the weather. All our nerves got edgy except Aunt Alma's. Nothing ever upset Aunt Alma. She prided herself a bit on that.

On Saturday the weather wound up with a regular downpour and a wind that rushed out of the black-green pines to lash the Wigwam and then rushed back like a maddened animal. The air was as full of torn, flying leaves as of rain, and the lake was a splutter of tossing waves. This charming day ended in a dank, streaming night.

And yet things had seemed a bit better than any day yet. Anthony was away. He had got some mysterious telegram just after breakfast, had taken the small motorboat, and gone to the mainland. I was thankful, for I felt I could no longer endure seeing a man's soul tortured as his was. Brenda had kept to her room all day on the good old plea of a headache. I won't say it wasn't a relief. We all felt the strain between her and Anthony like a tangible thing.

"Something — *something* — is going to happen," Madeline kept saying to me. She was really worse than the parrot.

After dinner we all gathered around the fireplace in the hall, where a cheerful fire of white birchwood was glowing; for although it was June the evening was cold. I settled back with a sigh of relief. After all, nothing lasted forever, and this infernal house party would be over on Monday. Besides, it was really quite comfortable and cheerful here, despite rattling windows and wailing winds and rainswept panes. Madeline turned out the electric lights, and the firelight was kind to the women, who all looked quite charming. Some of the Bright Young Things sat cross-legged on the floor with arms around one another quite indiscriminately as far as sex was concerned . . . except one languid, sophisticated creature in orange velvet and long amber earrings, who sat on a low stool with a lapful of silken housekeeper's cat, giving everyone an excellent view of the bones of her spine. Min's dog posed haughtily on the rug, and the parrot in his cage was quiet — for him — only telling us once in a while that he or someone else was devilish clever. Mrs. Howey, the housekeeper, insisted on keeping him in the hall, and Madeline had to wink at it because it was hard to get a housekeeper in Muskoka even for a Wigwam.

The Judge was looking like a chuckle because he had solved a jigsaw puzzle that had baffled everyone, and the Professor and Senator, who had been arguing stormily all day, were basking in each other's regard for a foeman worthy of his steel. Consuelo was sitting still, as usual. Mrs. Tennant and Aunt Alma were knitting pullovers. Kittens, her fat hands folded across her satin stomach, was surveying her Senator adoringly, and Miss Nosey was taking everything in. We were, for the time being, a contented, congenial bunch of people, and I did not see why Madeline should have suddenly proposed that each of us tell a ghost story, but she did. It was an ideal night for ghost stories, she averred. She hadn't heard any for ages and she understood that everybody had had at least one supernatural occurrence in his or her life.

"I suppose," said Professor Tennant a little belligerently, "that you would call anyone an ass who believed in ghosts?"

The Judge carefully fitted his fingertips together before he replied. "Oh, dear, no. I would not so insult asses."

"Of course if you don't *believe* in ghosts they can't happen," said Consuelo.

"Some people are able to see ghosts and some are not," announced Dick Lane. "It's simply a gift."

"A gift I was not dowered with," said Kittens complacently.

Mary Harland shuddered. "What a dreadful thing it would be if the dead really came back!"

"From ghoulies and ghaisties and langlegged beasties. And things that go bump in the night. Good Lord, deliver us," quoted Ted flippantly.

But Madeline was not to be sidetracked. Her little elfish face, under its crown of russet hair, was alive with determination.

"We're going to spook a bit," she said resolutely. "This is just the sort of night for ghosts to walk. Only of course they can't walk here because the Wigwam isn't haunted, I'm sorry to say. Wouldn't it be heavenly to live in a haunted house? Come now, everyone must tell a ghost story. Professor Tennant, you lead off. Something nice and creepy, please."

To my surprise, the Professor did lead off, although Mrs. Tennant's expression plainly informed us that she didn't approve of juggling with ghosts. He told a very good story too—punctuated with snorts from the Judge —about a house he knew which had been haunted by the voice of a dead child who joined in every conversation bitterly and vindictively. The child had, of course, been ill-treated and murdered, and its body was eventually found under the hearth-stone of the library. Then Dick told a tale about a dead dog that avenged its master, and Consuelo amazed me by spinning a really gruesome yarn of a ghost who came to the wedding of her lover with her rival . . . Consuelo said she knew the people. Ted knew a house in which you heard voices and footfalls where no voices or footfalls could be, and even Aunt Alma told of "a white lady with a cold hand" who asked you to dance with her. If you were reckless enough to accept the invitation you never lost the feeling of her cold hand in yours. This chilly apparition was always garbed in the costume of the seventies.

"Fancy a ghost in a crinoline," giggled a Bright Young Thing.

Min Ingram, of all people, had seen a ghost and took it quite seriously.

"Well, show me a ghost and I'll believe in it," said the Judge, with another snort.

"Isn't he devilish clever?" croaked the parrot.

Just at this point, Brenda drifted downstairs and sat down behind us all, her tragic eyes burning out of her white face. I had a feeling that there, in that calm, untroubled scene, full of good-humoured, tolerably amused, commonplace people, a human heart was burning at the stake in agony.

Something fell over us with Brenda's coming. Min Ingram's dog suddenly whined and flattened himself out on the rug. It occurred to me that it was the first time I had ever seen him looking like a real dog. I wondered idly what had frightened him. The housekeeper's cat sat up, its back bristling, slid from the orange velvet lap and slunk out of the hall. I had a queer sensation in the roots of what hair I had left, so I turned hastily to the slim, dark girl on the oak settle at my right.

"You haven't told us a ghost story yet, Christine. It's your turn."

Christine smiled. I saw the Judge look admiringly at her ankles, sheathed in chiffon hose. The Judge always had an eye for a pretty ankle. As for me, I was wondering why I couldn't recall Christine's last name and why I felt as if I had been impelled in some odd way to make that commonplace remark to her.

"Do you remember how firmly Aunt Elizabeth believed in ghosts?" said Christine. "And how angry it used to make her when I laughed at the idea? I am . . . wiser now."

"I remember," said the Senator in a dreamy way.

"It was your Aunt Elizabeth's money that went to the first Mrs. Armstrong, wasn't it?" said one of the Bright Young Things, nicknamed Tweezers. It was an abominable thing for anyone to say, right there before Brenda. But nobody seemed horrified. I had another odd feeling that it *had* to be said and who but Tweezers would say it? I had another feeling . . . that ever since Brenda's entrance every trifle was important, every tone was of profound significance, every word had a hidden meaning. Was I developing nerves?

"Yes," said Christine evenly.

"Do you suppose Susette Armstrong really took that overdose of chloral on purpose?" went on Tweezers unbelievably.

Not being near enough to Tweezers to assassinate her, I looked at Brenda. But Brenda gave no sign of having heard. She was staring fixedly at Christine.

"No," said Christine. I wondered how she knew, but there was no question whatsoever in my mind that she did know it. She spoke as one having authority. "Susette had no intention of dying. And yet she was doomed, although she never suspected it. She had an incurable disease which would have killed her in a few months. Nobody knew that except Anthony and me. And she had come to hate Anthony so. She was going to change her will the very next day—leave everything away from him. She told me so. I was furious. Anthony, who had spent his life doing good to suffering creatures, was to be left poor and struggling again, after his practice had been all shot to pieces by Susette's goings-on. I had loved Anthony ever since I had known him. He didn't know it—but Susette did. Trust her for that. She used to twit me with it. Not that it mattered . . . I knew he would never care for me. But I saw my chance to do something for him and I took it. I gave Susette that overdose of chloral. I loved him enough for that . . . and for *this*."

Somebody screamed. I have never known whether it was Brenda or not. Aunt Alma—who was never upset over anything—was huddled in her chair in hysterics. Kittens, her fat figure shaking, was clinging to her Senator, whose foolish, amiable face was grey—absolutely grey. Min Ingram was on her knees and the Judge was trying to keep his hands from shaking by clenching them together. His lips were moving and I know I caught the word, "God." As for Tweezers and all the rest of her gang, they were no longer Bright Young Things but simply shivering, terrified children.

I felt sick — very, very sick. *Because there was no one on the oak settle and none of us had ever known or heard of the girl I had called Christine.*

At that moment the hall door opened, a dripping Anthony entered. Brenda flung herself hungrily against him, wet as he was.

"Anthony . . . Anthony, forgive me," she sobbed.

Something good to see came into Anthony's worn face.

"Have you been frightened, darling?" he said tenderly. "I'm sorry I was so late. There was really no danger. I waited to get an answer to my wire to Los Angeles. You see I got word this morning that Christine Latham had been killed in a motor accident yesterday evening. She was Susette's second cousin and nurse . . . a dear, loyal little thing. I was very fond of her. I'm sorry you've had such an anxious evening, sweetheart."

August

Garfield Reeves-Stevens

If you've seen the jackets of Gar Reeves-Stevens's novels, you've seen the publicity photos of him: young, tall, fanatically clean-cut, forbidding. (Not someone you'd let feed the cats if you were out of town for the weekend.)

Read the novels and you'll come to the same conclusion. His characters as often as not come to violent, gooey ends. (You'd expect to come back to a home decorated with cat entrails.)

It's all a front. Gar is the sort of person who buys Girl Guide cookies—and then eats them! Gar wears sweatshirts with Mickey Mouse on them, bought during his monthly visit to Disneyland. He only helps old ladies across the street when they want to be helped across the street.

The tough-guy image is a complete fake. Not that you'd know it from this story.

I

It is August when what remains of our son comes to us for the first time. August, the hated month of still heat and windless nights, of wavering suns and the lonesome whine of unseen insects from beneath the dry pale grass crackling in flames by the roadside. The choking blackness of the burning gasoline seethes among the swollen green leaves of plants that have grown their fill, fulfilled their promise, with nothing now left to do but pause, motionless beneath the sun, within the heat, to wait for

14

the frost's shards, the snow's suffocation, and the winter's long night. August, when the promise of life proves hollow, when tires squeal on soft asphalt and brakes lock and cars arc through still air, with nothing now left to do but pause, motionless beneath the sun, within the heat, to crumple to the ground in shards, in suffocating heat and smoke, and take our son from us. And it is August when he comes back.

II

It is August and the heat is suffocating in my father's house, old in his time, older in ours, planned to be older still when the time would come for us to see our own son live within it. The time that was taken from us.

In this heat, in this stillness of the air from which no breath can be taken, we sleep in the basement, where the coolness of the earth presses in on the wood-panelled walls and brings us release. There is a couch there, from someone else's time, where we sleep, my wife and I, in the long still nights. When he was a baby, our son slept here, too, in August; the crib beside us, we would watch him in the soft glow of moonshine that silently entered through the high ground-level windows, and together, my wife and I, we would know that in him was our beginning and our end. With him, we knew, we were complete.

We cared for our son with that knowledge, honoured him with it, kept him safe with our love and our concern. In the winter, he was snug beneath extra blankets in his nursery. In the spring, he was dry beneath yellow slickers and high black boots in his yard. In August, he joined us in the coolness of the basement for the still, quiet nights. In August, we strapped him safely into his padded carseat for the long vacation drive along summer-softened roads bordered by layers of dry pale grass so eager for the cool and hot soaking embrace of flaming gasoline.

In August, our son still joins us in the coolness of the basement. For the still, quiet nights.

III

The first time, I am not sleeping. I lie beside my wife, so perfect, so ageless, the heart forever joined with mine, and I watch the soft pale glow of the moonshine as it steals across her, a caress of light as gentle as our love. In this moment, I am not sleeping, as if awakened by a sound or a signal sensed beneath conscious thought. A new light wars with the moonshine as a door opens into the wood-panelled room. I turn to it, silently, not to disturb her. There is a small hand on the doorknob facing out to the basement hall. The small hand pushes the door open wider. It is our son, what is left of him, coming into our room.

I can say nothing. I am not sleeping. My wife's clear eyes are open and I know she sees him, too. He is our son, come back to us, but different. He stands, tiny, lost, swamped by the light from the hallway behind him that sweeps over him and casts his features in shadow. I think of shadows in the heat of the hated August sun. Shadows and shade. The shade of our son has come to us. Respite from the heat, the hollow promises of life, the flames and heat of August. But he looks at us and looks past us and does not see us. He wanders into the basement room, darkened eyes and face looking all around, a plaintive search for something once lost, a favourite toy, a thing of the heart. But he doesn't find it. In the night and the soft silent glow of the moonshine I hold out my hand to him, to call him back to us, but he looks away and turns to the hall, and when he leaves, the door shuts softly behind him.

We listen carefully, our breath caught and silent, but we hear no footfalls, no scuffing of those tiny feet. Our son had come back to us and now he has left again and we are alone in the damp coolness, with nothing to do but wait.

IV

It is August again and again. The heat returns, the still air hangs round us, the basement offers coolness and something else we cannot discuss. It is August and we wait in the stillness and the silence and the cool pressing darkness for that door to open. And it does.

Our son comes to us again and again, with a terrible cruelty to his visits. His silent search remains the same. The door glides open, he takes his tentative steps, and his darkened, unseen eyes search the moonshine and the shadows enwrapped within the wood-panelled walls and still he cannot find what he is looking for.

We call out to him. We cry for him. We wave our hands and try to pull him to us to reclaim him as our own with each visit. But it is August, the hated month, and our hands slip through him as smoothly as the choking blackness of burning gasoline seethes among the swollen green leaves of plants that have grown their fill and have nowhere else to grow.

His unseeing eyes peer through us on our couch, the shade of August cast both ways, and again and again he looks away and turns back to the hall and its blinding light and the door shuts softly behind him.

We hear nothing more beyond, sense nothing more beyond. Except the waiting of life unfulfilled. Except the waiting.

V

It is August and we no longer seek the basement for its coolness. It is August and we no longer seek escape from the stillness and the heat. It is August and what is left of our son will come to us and for that alone we wait. In the basement.

Each time now the torment is worse because in some mad way our dreams have been torn from us to be used against us. Once, our son was protected in his crib, safe from the heat, beside us in this basement. We would look at him in the softness of the moonshine and we would yearn to know his future. To see him grow up healthy and strong, to see him become a man, a person, of whom we could be proud, a man, a person, who would take this house and become its master in his turn. In the softness of the moonshine we did not see him taken from us, safe in his padded chair, in a car undone by August, a car whose tires slipped, whose engine raced, which stayed a moment in the air then crumpled to the ground in shards and suffocation, taking him from us.

Yet those dreams are come to life before us, and our hearts threaten to be forever silent within us because of what we see.

It is August and what remains of our son is fuelled by our dreams to the point when we must wonder if it is still our son who comes to us. Before our eyes he has become a man, a person, tall and unbent, though still

washed by the shadows from the lights in the hall. It is
August and we see what has been taken from us, not
just the loss of the moment but the loss of all that was to
come. Our son was taken from us by August. And now
we know that month took from us our dreams and our
future as well.

We reach out to him, we call to him, we will him back
to be what was taken from us, but his eyes do not see,
his ears do not hear, trapped in his invariable routine,
he enters our room, he searches without success, and he
leaves. Tearing our hearts from us as he goes.

It is August.

VI

It is August and we no longer awaken just before the
door is to open. We have learned, we are ready. It is
always the same time. It is always the same thing. It is
August and what remains of our son is to return to us.
And so often has he done so that we no longer feel fear
at his appearance, we no longer feel anguish over our
lost dreams, we no longer feel sadness at his inevitable
departure. It is August and all that we can feel has been
taken from us, except the waiting for the door to open.
Except the waiting.

The door opens. The hand that propels it is our son's
hand, the nightmare hand we have seen grow and age
and wrinkle like a sheet of paper consumed by the fire
in the pale dry grass. We make no sound, we make no
movement. We wait for his search to play itself out again.
But this time, it does not.

Our son stands blinking in the doorway, looking
around the wood-panelled room. He walks ahead,

slowly, shambling, to the left, then the right, eyes searching as always before. Then we realize that we can see his
eyes. The shadows from the hallway light are still there,
but for the first time our son has stepped into the soft,
silent moonshine. I gaze at his face, seeing it at last.
Seeing the dreams I have lost to it with each wrinkle,
each twist, each scar and tuft of hair and beard. And my
son gazes back at me and holds my eyes with his.

This is different.

He nods at me, painfully, slowly. Nods at his mother,
my wife.

I reach out my hand to pass through him. It finds his
own. Real. Solid. The same as we are.

"It's all right now, Father," our son says. "I'm dead,
now, too."

He joins us here, within the pressing coolness of the
walls, away from the stillness and the heat and the flames
of August. He joins us and together we wait in the
silence, staring at the door, with nothing to do but wait
for it to open. With nothing to do but know that there is
no one left to open it.

VII

It is August. It is always August, now.

Coffins for Two

Vincent Starrett

"Vincent Starrett?" you may ask. He spent most of his life in Chicago and wrote as if he had spent his entire life in nineteenth-century Cambridge, England. How does he qualify for inclusion in this book? Well, he was born in Toronto in 1886, although he spent most of his eighty-eight years elsewhere.

Knowing that a quirky romp like "Coffins for Two" exists, how could we not include it? This is the ghost story that Poe would have written if Poe wrote tongue-in-cheek ghost stories. The language alone is worth savouring: "They fell upon each other with amenable fury; they hustled each other with the utmost cordiality."

Included in an obscure anthology by a Wisconsin publisher in 1965, this story is a tribute to Lynne's ability as a literary bloodhound.

About five o'clock of a foggy evening in late autumn, a man turned out of a side street in London, and with that fortuitousness which always surprises one in retrospect, collided with a second man headed in the opposite direction. Immediately, there was an outcry.

"Noakes!" exclaimed the first man.

The other man said: "Kirton!"

They fell upon each other with amenable fury; they hustled each other with the utmost cordiality.

"My dear fellow!" cried the man called Kirton, "it's twenty years since . . . !"

21

"All of that," agreed Noakes, happily, "but you are the same old rascal!"

"Nothing could change you but prosperity!" laughed Kirton.

"Then," said Noakes, irreverently, "I am the same yesterday, today and forever!"

There followed further affectionate insolences. Their conversation bristled with jovial exclamation points.

"Look here," said Kirton, at length, "we can't block-ade traffic in this fashion, old chap! I know an excellent tea-shop in the next square. I don't know how you feel about it, but I want to talk."

They linked arms, and countermarched crazily, to the delight of passersby; then aiming their sticks for a given point they swung away at a brisk walk.

A girl giggled her amusement. "And they say men don't gush!" she remarked to her companion.

The tea-shop looked inviting after the foggy street. Dimly revealed by a pattern of many-coloured oriental lamps, were divan-furnished corners, for the most part occupied by rapt specimens of the immortal twosome.

The reunited friends chose a corner at the farthest end, lattice-screened, and happily empty.

A Fatima in what was supposed to be Turkish costume hastened to their table. Her fat comeliness was re-assuring.

"Quite a place, eh," smiled Kirton. To the waitress he said: "Russian tea for two, and cigarettes."

His ease and familiarity suggested that, at least, he had been born in the place.

"Where have you been?" he continued, heartily.

"Oh, up and down the world!"

"It has many ups and downs."

"I've seen them all," laughed Noakes. "And you?"

"I, too, have them catalogued, although I haven't stirred out of London. I'm scribbling!"

"Not really? But you always had a turn that way, I remember."

"And you for adventure! I should not be surprised if we could collaborate to advantage. No doubt you have had some queer experiences."

"Queer! My dear fellow, the mildest thing I have seen is twenty Chinamen beheaded in as many minutes! The wildest . . . well, I once came close to marrying for money!"

Kirton roared. "Oh, excellent!" he said. "But I take it that you are not now married?"

"No, and you, of course, are still . . . ? I should have thought so! Well, well, as we grow older . . . !"

"Yes," agreed Kirton, "and we are certainly growing no younger. Damnation, but it is good to see you again! A light, old fellow!"

Their cigarette tips met in the masculine kiss of fire.

"Do you remember our parting, twenty years ago? . . . Ridiculous!"

"Absurd!" said Noakes. "By the way, what became of her?"

Kirton shrugged expressively. "Dance hall," he said, "and now a star of the first magnitude. Her name is up in electric lights."

"The deuce it is! I should like to see the lights, at least. I used to think of her a good deal, when I was in America. I even imagined *you* as married to her. I say, we might take in the show, Kirton!"

"We might," admitted Kirton, without enthusiasm, "but why revive old memories? We are happier as we are."

"I suppose so; yet, I confess I should like to see her. By Jove, she hit me hard, old man! I used to think she was pretty fond of me, until you showed up. After that, I had no chance."

"I'm afraid you flatter me," said Kirton, dryly.

"Well, she *did* throw you down, too, of course! I was tickled at the time; thought it portended ineffable things, and all that rot! But it didn't." He coughed. "I had a letter from her, after I'd cleared out. I thought she was a bit sorry, but when it came I was tied down."

"A letter! So did I!"

"The devil! Say, she *was* playing a game, wasn't she?"

"Or is!" said Kirton, in a voice suddenly hard. "Look here, Noakes, when did you get that letter?"

"Well," said Noakes, teasingly, "you may as well know it first as last, old man! I had it just before I sailed. I left America on the first boat. I knew nothing of her present position, and I'm blessed if I know how she knew my address."

Kirton slowly rose to his feet. "And you are on your way to her?"

"Why not?"

"Noakes," whispered Kirton, "I received my letter two weeks ago, also fixing this date for our meeting! I was on my way to her when I met you. I am due in less than an hour."

They stared at each other across the little table. Their animosity was scarcely veiled. The lips of Kirton curled in a slow sneer.

"Noakes," he intoned, "you are not going!"

Noakes leaned back in his chair to relieve the tension. He caught his breath and spoke calmly.

"Yes," he said, "I am going!"

Suddenly, Kirton was off in a fit of sardonic laughter.

"They don't do it better on the stage," he said. "There's no use of going on like this, Noakes. We're getting old, and she's been married twice. Fools! Old fools! And yet we both want her! We are good enough for her now, and so she writes . . . and we crawl to her on our bellies! We are deluded by a mirage of happiness after a hell of renunciation. Knowing which, we want her! Noakes, one of us has got to quit. Will you gamble for her?"

Noakes was silent for a moment.

"No!" he said, at length. "If one of us quits, Kirton, he's got to *quit*!"

Again they stared, this time fearfully. Kirton reseated himself as slowly as he had risen.

"All right," he said, after a moment. "How?"

"In my experiences beyond London," said Noakes, "I learned many curious things. Among them is an infallible remedy for the fever of living. This is it!"

From a vest pocket he drew forth a small vial filled with a colourless liquid.

The plump Fatima entered the booth.

"Fresh tea!" ordered Noakes, replying to her smile.

The tea was placed before them.

"Three drops," said Noakes, "should be enough."

Silently, they looked at the fatal cup.

"How shall we juggle them?" inquired Kirton.

"It is simple," replied Noakes. "I shall leave the room, while you shift them about. When I return, you shall leave the room, and I shall shift them. You see, there is no difference in their appearance."

"Very well," said Kirton.

Noakes arose and left the room. Kirton could hear him chatting and laughing with the *pulchritudinous houri.*

From an inner pocket, Kirton extracted an envelope, and from the envelope a folded paper. Into the untouched cup he quickly shook a white powder, and gently stirred the tea until the powder was dissolved. Then, rapidly, he shifted the cups a number of times, and went after Noakes. They exchanged occupations.

At his friend's call, Kirton returned. Hate shone in the eyes of each as they faced across the table.

"May the best man win!" murmured Noakes, tritely, picking up his cup.

"And huzza for the next man who dies!" quoted Kirton, with his mind upon a name in electric letters.

They drained the small cups at a gulp.

"How fast does it operate?" inquired Kirton, casually.

"Oh, say five minutes," replied Noakes. "It is very gentle; no violent gripings. You will simply fall asleep."

"I? Why do you assume that I have drawn the cup?"

"I had marked my own by a tiny chip in the handle. You would have drawn it in any case, you see! I am sorry, Kirton, but . . . !"

He shrugged eloquently. Kirton peacefully smiled.

"I suspected something of the sort," he admitted. "While you were absent, I shook a powder into your cup, Noakes. It acts in perhaps five minutes, and is very gentle. You will seem to fall asleep."

Noakes straightened and looked keenly into his friend's face.

"You devil!" he cried, admiringly. "You did! I can see it in your eyes! So we are both to die? And together! We go out together! Damnation, Kirton, but I think I am glad!"

"And I!" said Kirton, gently. "Yes, it has turned out very well. We shall be better friends on the other side. Dear old chap!" he added, affectionately. "I had no letter, Noakes. That was a lie! I was jealous, though. I couldn't bear the thought of you going to her; to think that she had sent for you! I was on my way to the club, old man, when you met me, where I had planned to take the powder myself. I was a bit tired of it all! Will you forgive me?"

"Forgive you!" cried Noakes, feebly. "There is nothing to forgive. I, too, lied about the letter. She never wrote me, Kirton! She always cared more for you."

"No," insisted Kirton, "it was you she favoured, Noakes."

Noakes smiled and settled down more deeply in his chair.

"She cared for neither of us," he said, faintly. "We are two old fools, Kirton, to murder each other for a hussy who would not spit upon either of us and who is not worth spittle. *Au revoir*, old fellow!"

'For a few . . . moments . . . ," breathed Kirton.

"My Gawd!" said Fatima to the police officer who took her testimony a half hour later. "They fought about a woman who threw them both down! I heard enough of it, sir! My Gawd! And the world full of women, and some of 'em close at hand!"

Two ghosts entered a fashionable undertaking parlour, shortly after six o'clock, and proceeded arm in arm, in the most affectionate manner, to the desk, where they bowed politely to the surprised manager.

"Coffins for two!" they chuckled in unison, and tapping the astonished man upon the wrist with their canes, they fled out into the dusk like truant schoolboys.

The Money Box

Elaine Driedger

I first met Elaine Driedger when I was a guest editor at the first Waterloo Mystery Writers' Conference in 1985. She shyly approached me during a coffee break, saying she didn't think that her writing was ready to be read by all of these Real Writers, and anyway it wasn't a mystery story, but would I mind letting her know what I thought. Inevitably, it was the best thing I read during the whole conference.

Elaine's writing is always subtle enough that your immediate reaction is to go straight back to the beginning of the story and reread it, to see how she managed to make it end up where it did. She creates memorable characters with very few words; Chester in "The Money Box" is a good example.

In 1985, Seal Books sponsored Elaine for an Ontario Arts Council grant to encourage her with her writing. This is the first time we've had the pleasure of publishing her.

She hadn't been out to the cemetery for more than a week. He realized now that he'd been uneasy about it. She hadn't missed since April, even when it was cold. He'd wondered if she'd been sick or . . . but she was there today, rooting around in the petunia bed, her hoe and rake scattered on the lawn behind her.

Doing more harm than good like as not, he thought. I should've known she'd be back, the old pest.

He figured he shouldn't stop the tractor today. He was getting behind with the cultivating. He was a busy man, wasn't he? A hundred acres to look after all on his own.

A man like that couldn't be expected to drop what he was doing and stand chatting in a cemetery in the middle of a good working day.

From his jostling seat, he watched her pull some long weeds from the middle of the bed. Her skirt flapped in the breeze between spread legs. Some of her grey hair had come loose and drifted gently around her head. She wore bright yellow rubber gloves. Above them, the skin of her arms sagged with age.

Chester glanced down just in time to see the corn row end beneath his tractor. He sprang onto the clutch to keep the nose of his machine from hitting the cemetery fence. He shut the ignition off and sighed.

Uncurling her thin body, Maria swept some weeds into an arc that sent them flying, dirt-clotted roots first, into Chester's field. She turned and smiled at him still sitting on his tractor. Rising from the flowerbed, she pulled off her gloves and bent to pick up a wicker basket covered with a faded pink cloth, cross-stitched with purple pansies.

Chester was pleased to see the basket, but he didn't move. Maria walked towards him and smiled again.

"Like some coffee? I brought fresh buns today. Just baked them this morning." She raised the basket a few inches towards him.

Perspiration trickled from Chester's armpits down his sides and into his shirt. "Well, I suppose a man needs a rest, too, though how I'll get all the work done this month I couldn't tell you. But a man's got to make a living somehow." He heaved himself from the tractor seat, landed heavily on a dusty furrow, and quickly followed Maria around the fence to the shade of a thick old maple growing in the ditch bank.

"You work too hard, Chester." Maria glanced at him.

"And you worry too much. The Lord'll give you strength and time enough."

Chester shivered with a sudden suspicion. "Humph!" He plopped himself down on the neat cemetery lawn and watched Maria spread the cloth on the grass. She set out two china cups emblazoned with the rose of Sharon and filled them with steaming coffee from a rusting thermos. She always brought two cups now.

He smelled the yeastiness from the basket and shifted impatiently. Maria set a heaping plateful of the buns and a jar of cherry jam with a spoon stuck into it on the cloth beside the coffee cups. She rummaged in the basket again and pulled out a small jar of milk. She always brought milk, but no sugar. Chester preferred sugar, and he felt angry that she had never asked him about his tastes. She just poured a generous dollop into his coffee every time.

She'd come right into his yard one day, up the steps and knocked on the screen door. Needed a hoe. She'd forgotten hers and didn't want to walk all the way home to get it. She'd stood with her face pressed against the screen, her hand shading out the sunlight. Nosy old woman, he'd thought, but she'd reminded him more of a curious puppy. She hadn't seemed like the type who was looking around so she'd have some gossip to tell. Even so, he'd been uneasy. He'd hoped she wouldn't notice too much.

"You sure don't keep much around, do you," she'd blurted out after he'd unhooked the door for her. He'd almost jumped forward to push her out then, but he'd been able to control himself.

"I try to live simple. No point in fancy stuff. It just wastes your money."

Her eyes had lit up at that. ''Yes,'' she'd said. Then her face lost its puppy look. ''It's not good to waste money, but there are other things that are worse to waste.''

''Like what?'' he'd challenged.

''Oh, lots of things,'' she'd answered with a dreamy look. ''I think the worst, though, is to waste yourself.''

A tight smile had played over Chester's lips. He'd hurried her out then, to get the hoe in the barn before she could ask any questions, before she could find out more.

The breeze riffled through the leaves of the maple. Maria picked up a cup of milky coffee and held it out to Chester. When he reached for it, his fingers touched hers for a moment. He jerked away, slopping hot liquid over his hand. He set the cup down and rubbed a wrinkled bandanna over his reddening fingers. Maria held her own cup tight and did not look at him.

After her visit for the hoe, Maria had started waving to him whenever he'd been working the stretch of land edging the cemetery. None of the other caretakers had ever acknowledged his presence before, and so he knew that he would have to keep an eye on her.

He'd watched her whenever he could, but he hadn't stopped until mid-May, when the tractor had given him some trouble and he'd shut it off to look it over. Maria, leaning against the whitewashed fence, had offered him one of her little buns with a big lump of jam on it. He figured he'd better humour her. They hadn't talked much that day, but the next time Maria had brought an extra cup, and so he'd lingered at the fence, sipping the hot coffee.

He'd begun to feel peculiar after that, had had trouble

getting to sleep some nights. And for some reason, the field around the cemetery seemed in need of extra care this year. He knew it was partly because he'd begun avoiding it and letting it go. Then there was more to do when he did get to it, and with stopping for coffee every few days, it took that much longer. Still, it did seem unusually time-consuming to work in that field.

He knew now that this was all because of Maria. His whole life was getting mixed up and it was her fault. He didn't want someone throwing him off guard. With Maria he'd begun to feel for the first time in years that he was losing control. That was dangerous.

Chester stuffed the bandanna back into his pocket and picked up a fat, spongy bun. He broke it open, dropped a dollop of jam onto half of it, and shoved the whole piece into his mouth at once. Maria's bun had two neat bites out of it and her coffee cup stood two-thirds full. She always finished at exactly the same time he did. This had startled him at first because he never saw her actually chewing or drinking.

They ate in silence until there was only one bun left.

"Your hand okay?" Maria asked. Chester glanced at her warily.

"Yeah, it was nothing. Just a little burn."

"Here, let me take a look at it." Maria leaned towards him.

Cautiously he put his hand forward, but she didn't touch it. He was relieved. He didn't want to feel her strange, cold fingers again.

She peered for a long time at his palm, her head bent much closer than seemed necessary. Near-sighted as a mole going blind, for pete's sakes, he thought. But he didn't pull away. Her presence held him in a deep calmness like the shelter of a barn when a blizzard is threatening.

She leaned back reluctantly and then jerked her head away as though she'd remembered something frightening. She began to gather the cups, plate, and milk jar, her hands darting about, her head turned down. She chucked the items into her basket. Chester had never seen her work this quickly. She was usually awkward and slow.

They rose together, knees cracking, from the shady lawn and tramped heavily to the gap in the fence corner. The headstones of the cemetery were all flat, rectangular slabs imbedded in the earth so that a mower could run right over them. From a distance the graveyard looked more like a simple, well-kept park laced with flowerbeds and dotted with bouquets left by family members.

Chester never liked the walk through the cemetery. Stepping over top of dead strangers made him feel adrift and unprotected. He felt that way in other places, too— at the bank, in the grocery store. The world seemed full of dead strangers. He went to these places as little as possible. After his visits with Maria he was always glad to get back into his tractor seat, though the feeling came to him there sometimes, too. It was at home, with the money, his money, that he felt most in control. There the feeling was almost squelched.

"Doesn't it bother you to work here?" he asked suddenly. He felt bolder with her today. He had begun to wonder what she was thinking.

Her face grew puzzled, then cleared. "Oh, you mean because it's a cemetery." She shrugged. "No, I guess I don't think about it much. It's only the bodies we put here. The souls go to heaven to be with the Lord." She said it simply, as though it was something she'd been told and was repeating to him. He liked how her face looked when she said it. There was something firm and immovable in her eyes. It reminded him of his mother.

He stopped at the fence and looked back at her. The wind tossed her loosened hair into a halo-like covering. He was struck with a sense of something new yet familiar. The feeling passed, and he abruptly mounted his tractor.

"Thanks for the coffee," he grunted and yanked ruthlessly at the starter. He had to get away now. He swerved his machine into a new furrow. She usually called out "See you tomorrow," but today he didn't hear her. He wanted very much to look back, but he didn't.

When Chester stomped out of the barn shortly after seven o'clock that evening, he realized something was wrong. The rotting bottom step of the back porch that he'd been meaning to fix had broken through. His gaze swept over the porch and screen door. A cold, turning lump coursed through his body. The inner door was slanting in away from the screen.

He slammed into the kitchen, sending plaster loose with the jarring doorknob. A howl broke animal-like from his throat and shrieked through the stillness of the raped house.

Chester ignored the littered floor, the gaping cupboards retched clean of contents. Like a wounded man he lurched through the kitchen doorway and up the stairs. In his bedroom, a window full of evening glare at first hid from him the sifted, ransacked drawers and chests. His eyes, adjusting to the light, took in the horror. On the floor, pulled out from under the bed, lay a small wooden box, its lid flung back like the head of a dead thing.

Chester fell on the box, his hands sliding and probing

along the inner walls of the little case, his breath twittering with the high-pitched sobs of a child. His hands grew still. With awkward tenderness, he shut the lid and took the box into his arms, cradling it against his heaving chest.

The flaming evening passed and darkness enclosed him as he sat.

"They've found me," he thought. "They couldn't leave me be. No, they've got to destroy me." His body trembled. "Damn them, will they never be finished? Will they never be satisfied? Not till I'm dead, not till I'm dead and buried."

His pain, ripping through the core of his body, had not been like this, not this unbearable, since that last day, thirty-seven years ago, when his father had said, "Leave!" His brothers had stood there behind him, staring as though Chester no longer existed. And of course for them he didn't. His mother, their father's wife, the only link that had tied him to them, was dead.

Chester shoved the box back under the bed and dragged himself from the floor. His legs quaked from his long kneeling. A cooling flow of night air from the open window fluttered over his damp skin. He turned with a cry and slammed the sash down. Plunging through the house, he clutched other windows shut and crashed doors fast. When he'd sealed the place tight, he let go of the panic a little.

He knew they'd been watching him, hunting him. They had never left him with anything — the stick of Christmas candy, the gleaming new jack-knife. He'd find things missing and see a sly grin steal over Jake's or Abe's face. Later he'd see Abe whittling with the missing knife.

Their eyes would lock in a tug-of-war until Chester would turn and walk away. He was the outsider, the one who'd had a different mother.

Chester slumped down on a chair at the kitchen table, laid his head on his folded arms and wept.

Over the next week, a typical midsummer heat wave turned the sealed house into a sweatbox. Chester lay most of the day on the bed upstairs or on the lumpy cushions of the sofa in the living room, staring at a wall or ceiling. Some part of his body always moved — index fingers pressing against thumbs, toes curling and uncurling, teeth chewing tongue and lips. Already on the evening of the theft he had made the connection — the money had been taken while he'd been in the cemetery with Maria. She had been sent to spy on him. The plan, as he saw it now, had been so simple, so obvious. He hadn't given her any information, he was sure of that, but he'd let his guard down. That's all they'd needed.

He couldn't eat. He wasn't a drinking man, but the bottle of whisky he kept on hand was gone after two days and he wouldn't leave the house to get more. His unwashed body lay clothed in its own decaying odour. He wondered what death would smell like.

He wanted to hate her, to scream curses at the memory of her — grey, wispy hair, cotton skirts slapping in the wind. She would not leave him. At night — in spare moments of sleep — she walked through his dreams, alone at first, then later, with another figure glowing angel-like. The third time they appeared he knew that the other figure was his mother.

Something began to build inside him. He tried to fight it. He stared for hours at a spot on the ceiling, counted squares of linoleum on the floor, closed his eyes, and tried to think of nothing. The distractions worked for a while. He knew that ultimately they would fail.

"Maria," he screamed at last against the tight windows, the locked, immovable doors. "Maria!" He wept, kneeling on the floor. The sound of her name was sucked into the pressured corners of the house, swallowed whole without an echo.

Footsteps. He jerked his head up. A rattle of knocks at the back door.

"Chester, Chester! You all right?" The words were mangled in panic. "Chester, are you in there? Open up."

She's come back, he thought. She's found a way to sneak the money from them. She's bringing it back.

He hurled to the door, wrenched the knob, and swung back. A cry gurgled from his throat.

Hot wind from the empty yard swept over his sweaty body. He'd heard her. She'd knocked and called out. He knew he hadn't imagined it. He could feel her presence as something drifting quietly away.

Who was she? Chester's stomach quivered. He'd been afraid to ask that question, he realized. He'd been steering away from the idea that she was more than just an old woman tending flowers at a cemetery.

"But why me? What does she want with me?"

The heat wave broke that night with a thunderstorm. Chester opened all of the windows and let the moist air wash through the house. He discovered very little missing or broken as he went about picking up and clearing away. The thieves had been looking for something and they'd found it.

He could think about them now, whoever they were.

He no longer felt as though they were sitting on his chest, trying to strangle his throat.

He went into town the next day. The trees shimmered with the gleam of last night's rain. His fields, as he passed them, looked well tended and bright with growth.

With difficulty he reported the robbery at the police station. He was embarrassed to explain that he had discovered the money missing seven days ago. Why hadn't he come in sooner? By this time there was little chance of tracing anything. It was really too bad. The sergeant shook his head. "People don't cooperate and then they expect miracles. I don't give you any hope that we can solve this."

Chester smiled. He did not doubt that they would not solve it. He had come only because of the little part of his belief that had not been won over. It was a sort of fleece to test the finality of his decision. He hoped they never found the money.

Out on the street Chester turned towards the grocery store. A small, neat woman in her late fifties caught his eye. He had never seen her before. She smiled. Chester smiled back and walked whistling down the street.

The Charlottetown Banquet

Robertson Davies

Who has ever looked at a photograph of Robertson Davies and not imagined him slurping soup through that wonderful moustache?

It is the food that stars in "The Charlottetown Banquet." As John A. Macdonald rambles on about the Great Exposition of 1851, your head is full of images of partridges and wild duck. He discusses deficits, you dream of the taste of Genoa Creams.

This is not in any way to suggest that any of Davies' wonderful story is dull. Rather, no matter how engrossing a dinner conversation may be, if the food is good enough the conversation becomes something of a side dish. This story leaves a lingering aftertaste of sherry.

The range of guests who come to our fortnightly High Table dinners is wide, and provides us with extraordinarily good company. Sometimes we get a surprise—an economist who turns out to be a poet, for instance. (I mean a poet in the formal sense: all economists are rapt, fanciful creatures; it is necessary to their profession.) Only last Friday we had a visitor whom I found a most delightful and illuminating companion. I shall not tell you what his profession is, or you will immediately identify him, and I shall have betrayed his secret, which is that he is a medium.

He does not like being a medium. He finds it embarrassing. But the gift, like being double-jointed or having the power to wiggle one's ears, can neither be acquired by study nor abdicated by an act of will. His particular power lies in the realm of psychometry; that is to say that sometimes — not always — he finds that when he is near to an object that has strong and remarkable associations, he becomes aware of those associations with an intensity that is troublesome to him. And occasionally psychic manifestations follow.

He confided this to me just as we were leaving the small upstairs dining room, where we assemble after dinner for conversation and a reasonable consumption of port and Madeira. We were standing at the end of the room by the sideboard, for he had been looking at our College grant-of-arms; he put his hand on the wall to the left of the frame, to enable him to lean forward for a closer look, and then he turned to me, rather white around the mouth, I thought, and said —

"Let's go downstairs. It's terribly close in here."

I thought it was the cigar smoke that was troubling him. Excellent as the Bursar's cigars undoubtedly are, the combustion of a couple of dozen of them within an hour does make the air rather heavy. So I went downstairs with him, and thought no more about the matter.

It must have been a couple of hours later that I was taking a turn around the quad for a breath of air before bed, when I saw something I did not like. The window of the small dining room was lighted up, but not by electricity. It was a low, flickering light that seemed to rise and fall in its intensity, and I thought at once of fire. I dashed up the stairs with a burst of speed that any of the Junior Fellows might envy, and opened the door. Sure enough, there was light in the room.

But — ! Now you must understand that we had left the room in the usual sort of disorder; the table had been

covered with the debris of our frugal academic pleasures
— nutshells, the parings of fruit, soiled wine-glasses,
filled ashtrays, crumpled napkins, and all that sort of
thing. But now—!

I have never seen the room looking as it looked at that
moment. How shall I describe it?

To begin, the table was covered with a cloth of that
refulgent bluey-whiteness that speaks of the finest linen.
And, what is more, there was not a crease in it; obviously
it had been ironed on the table. The pattern that was
woven into it was of maple leaves, entwined with lilies
and roses. At every place — and it was set for twenty-
four — was a napkin folded into the intricate shape
known to Victorian butlers as Crown Imperial. At either
end of the table was a soup tureen, and my heightened
senses immediately discerned that the eastern tureen
contained Mock Turtle, while that at the western end
was filled with a Consommé enriched with a *julienne* of
truffles — that is to say, Consommé Britannia. A noble
boiled salmon of the Restigouche variety was displayed
on one platter, with a vessel of Lobster Sauce in waiting,
and on another was a selection of Fillets of the most
splendid Nova Scotia mackerel, each gleaming with the
pearls of a Sauce Maître d'Hôtel.

And the Entrées! Petites Bouches à la Reine, and
Grenadine de Veau with a Pique Sauce Tomate — and
none of your nasty bottled tomato sauce, either, but the
genuine fresh article. There was a Lapin Sauté which
had been made to stand upright, its paws raised as
though in delight at its own beauty, and a charming fluff
of cauliflower sprigs where its tail had been a few hours
before; you could see that it was served au Champi-
gnons, for two button mushrooms gleamed where its

eyes had once been. There was a Cotellete d'Agneau
with, naturally, Petits Pois. There was a Coquette de
Volaille, and a Timbale de Macaroni which had been
moulded into the form of—of all things—a Beaver.

In addition there were roasted turkeys, chickens, a
saddle of mutton, and a sirloin of beef, and there were
boiled turkeys, hams, corned beef, and mutton cutlets.
And it was all piping hot.

The flickering soft light I had seen through the window
came from a gasolier that hung over the table, and
through its alabaster globes gleamed the gaslight —
surely one of the loveliest forms of illumination ever
devised by man.

You have recognized the meal, of course. Every gour-
met has that menu by heart. It was the Grand Banquet in
Honour of the Colonial Delegates which was held at the
Halifax Hotel in Charlottetown on September 12, 1864.
This was the authentic food of Confederation. A specimen
of the menu, elegantly printed on silk, and the gift of
Professor Maurice Careless, one of our Senior Fellows,
hangs on the wall of our small dining room, just at the
point where our guest, the medium, had laid his hand.

Nor was this all. What I have described to you at some
length leapt at my eye in an instant, and my gaze had
turned to the sideboard, which was laden with bottles of
wine.

And what bottles! Tears came into my eyes, just to
look at them. For these were not our ugly modern bottles,
with their disagreeable Government stickers adhering to
them, and their high shoulders, and their uniformity of
shape, and their self-righteous airs, as though in the half-
literate, nasal drone of politicians, they were declaiming:
'We are the support of paved roads, general education,

and public health; we are the pillars of society.' No, no; these were smaller bottles, in a multiplicity of shapes and colours. There were the slim pale-green maidens of hock; the darkly opalescent romantic ports; the sturdily gay clarets, and the high-nosed aristocrats of Burgundy; there were champagnes that almost danced, yet were not gassy impostors; and they were all bottles of the old shapes and the old colours—dark, merry, and wicked.

My knees gave a little, and I sat down in the nearest chair.

It was then that I noticed the figure by the sideboard. His back was towards me, and whether he was somewhat clouded in outline, or whether my eyes were dazzled by the table, I cannot say, but I could not quite make him out. He was hovering—I might almost say gloating—over a dozen of sherry. That should have given me a clue, but you will understand that I was not fully myself. And, furthermore, I had at that instant recalled that the menu given to us by Professor Careless was said by him to have been the property of the Honourable George Brown. On such a matter one does not doubt the word of Maurice Careless.

"Mr. Brown! I believe?" I said, in what I hoped was a hospitable tone.

"God forbid that I should cast doubt on any man's belief," said the figure, still with its back to me, "but I cannot claim the distinction you attribute to me." He picked up a bottle of sherry and drew the cork expertly. Then he drew the cork of another, and turned toward me with a wicked chuckle, a bottle in either hand;

"These are Clan Alpine's warriors true,
And, Saxon, I am Roderick Dhu—"

said he, and I was so astonished that I quite overlooked the disagreeable experience of being addressed as a Saxon. For it was none other than Old Tomorrow himself!

Yes, it was Sir John A. Macdonald in his habit as he lived. Or rather, not precisely as we are accustomed to seeing him, but in Victorian evening dress, with a red silk handkerchief thrust into the bosom of his waistcoat. But that head of somewhat stringy ringlets, that crumpled face which seemed to culminate and justify itself in the bulbous, coppery nose, that watery, rolling, merry eye, the accordion pleating of the throat, those moist, mobile lips, were unmistakable.

"If you were expecting Brown, I am truly sorry," he continued. "But, you see, I was the owner of this menu." (He pronounced it, in the Victorian manner, meenoo.) "Brown pocketed it as we left the table. It was a queer little way he had, of picking up odds and ends; we charitably assumed he took them home to his children. But it's mine, right enough. Look, you can see my thumbmark on it still."

But I was not interested in thumb-prints. I was deep in awe of the shade before me. I started to my feet. In a voice choking with emotion I cried: "The Father of my country!"

"Hookey Walker!" said Sir John, with a wink. "Tuck in your napkin, Doctor, and let us enjoy this admirable repast."

I had no will of my own. I make no excuses. Who, under such circumstances, would have done other than he was bidden? I sat. Sir John, with remarkable grace, uncovered the Mock Turtle, and gave me a full plate. I ate it. Then he gave me a plate of the Consommé Britannia.

I ate it. Then I had quite a lot of the salmon. Then a substantial helping of mackerel. I ate busily, humbly, patriotically.

I have always heard of the extraordinary gustatory zest of the Victorians. They ate hugely. But it began to be borne in upon me, as Sir John plied me with one good thing after another, that I was expected to eat all, or at least some, of everything on the table. My gorge rose. But, I said to myself, when will you, ever again, eat such a meal in such company? And my gorge subsided. I began to be aware that my appetite was unimpaired. The food I placed in my mouth, and chewed, and swallowed, seemed to lose substance somewhere just behind my necktie. I had no sense of repletion. And little by little it came upon me that I was eating a ghostly meal, in ghostly company, and that under such circumstances I could go on indefinitely. Not even my jaws ached. But the taste —ah, the taste was as palpable as though the viands were of this earth.

Meanwhile Sir John was keeping pace with me, bite for bite. But rather more than glass for glass. He had asked me to name my poison, which I took to be a Victorian jocularity for choosing my wine, and I had taken a Moselle—a fine Berncasteler—with the soup and fish, and had then changed to a St. Emilion with the entrées. (It was particularly good with the rabbit, a dish of which I am especially fond; Sir John did not want any, and I ate that rabbit right down to the ground, and sucked its ghostly bones.) But Sir John stuck to sherry. Never have I seen a man put away so much sherry. And none of your whimpering dry sherries, either, but a brown sherry that looked like liquefied plum pudding. He threw it off a glass at a time, and he got through bottle after bottle.

You must not suppose that we ate in silence. I do not report our conversation because it is of slight interest. Just — "Another slice of turkey, my dear Doctor; allow me to give you the liverwing." And — "Sir John, let me press you to a little more of this excellent Timbale de Macaroni; and may I refill your glass. Oh, you've done it yourself." You know the sort of thing; the polite exchanges of men who are busy with their food.

But at last the table was empty, except for bones and wreckage. I sat back, satisfied yet in no way uncomfortable, and reached for a toothpick. It was a Victorian table, and so there were toothpicks of the finest sort—real quill toothpicks such as one rarely sees in these weakly fastidious days. I was ready to put into effect the plan I had been hatching.

In the bad old days, before the academic life claimed me, I was, you must know, a journalist. And here I found myself in a situation of which no journalist would dare even to dream. Across the table from me sat one whose unique knowledge of our country's past was incalculably enhanced by his extraordinary privilege of possessing access to our country's future! Here was one who could tell me what would be the outcome of the present disquiet in Quebec. And then how I should be courted in Ottawa! Would I demand the Order of Canada—the Companionship, not the mere medal — before I deigned to reveal what I knew? And how I should lord it over Maurice Careless! But I at once put this unworthy thought from me. Whom the gods would destroy, they first make mad. I wound myself up to put my leading question.

But, poor creature of the twentieth century that I am, I was mistaken about the nature of our meal.

"Ready for the second course, I think, eh Doctor?"

said Sir John, and waved his hand. In a moment, in the twinkling of an eye—the biblical phrase popped into my mind—the table was completely reset, and before us was spread a profusion of partridges, wild duck, lobster salad, galantines, plum pudding, jelly, pink blancmange, Charlotte Russe, Italian Cream, a Bavarian Cream, a Genoa Cream, plates of pastries of every variety—apple puffs, bouchées, cornucopias, croquenbouche, flans, strawberry tartlets, maids-of-honour, stuffed monkeys, prune flory, tortelli—it was bewildering. And there were ice creams in the Victorian manner—vast temples of frozen, coloured, flavoured cornstarch—and there were plum cakes and that now forgotten delicacy called Pyramids.

And fruit! Great towers of fruit, mounting from foundations of apples, through oranges and nectarines to capitals of berries and currants, upon each of which was perched the elegantly explosive figure of a pineapple.

You see, I had forgotten that a proper Victorian dinner had a second course of this nature, so that one might have some relaxation after the serious eating was over.

But Sir John seemed disappointed. "What!" he cried; "no gooseberry fool? And I had been so much looking forward to it!" He proceeded to drown his sorrow in sherry.

I had no fault to find. I began again, eating methodically of every dish, and accepting second helpings of Charlotte Russe and plum cake. During this course I drank champagne only. It was that wonderful Victorian champagne, somewhat sweeter than is now fashionable, and with a caressing, rather than an aggressive, carbonization. I hope I did not drink greedily, but in Sir John's company it was not easy to tell.

I do not mean to give you the impression that Sir John

was the worse for his wine. He was completely self-possessed, but I could not help being aware that he had consumed nine bottles of sherry without any assistance from me, and that he showed no sign of stopping. I knew — once again I was in the debt of Professor Careless for this information—that it was sherry he had favoured for those Herculean bouts of solitary drinking that are part of his legend. I was concerned, and I suppose my concern showed. Before I could begin my interrogation, might not my companion lose the power of coherent speech? I sipped my champagne and nibbled abstractedly at a stuffed monkey, wondering what to do. Suddenly Sir John turned to me.

"Have a weed?" he said. I accepted an excellent cigar from the box he pushed towards me.

"And a b. and s. to top off with?" he continued. Once again I murmured my acquiescence, and he prepared a brandy and soda for me at the sideboard. But for himself he kept right on with the sherry.

"Now, Doctor," said Sir John, "I can see that you have something on your mind. Out with it."

"It isn't very easy to put into words," said I. "Here am I, just as Canada's centennial year is drawing to a close, sitting alone with the great architect of our Confederation. Naturally my mind is full of questions; the problem is, which should come first?"

"Ah, the centennial year," said Sir John. "Well, in my time, you know, we didn't have this habit of chopping history up into century-lengths. It's always the centennial of something."

"But not the centennial of Canada," said I. "You cannot pretend to be indifferent to the growth of the country you yourself brought into being."

"Not indifferent at all," said he. "I've put myself to no end of inconvenience during the past year, dodging all over the continent — *a mari usque ad mare* — to look at this, that, and the other thing."

I could not control myself; the inevitable question burst from my lips. "Did you see Expo?" I cried.

"I certainly did," said he, laughing heartily, "and I took special trouble to be there at the end when they were adding up the bill. The deficit was roughly eight times the total budget of this Dominion for the year 1867. You call that a great exposition? Why, my dear Doctor, the only Great Exposition that made any sense at all was the Great Exposition of 1851. It was the only world's fair in history that produced a profit. And why was that? Because it was dominated by that great financier and shrewd man of business Albert the Prince Consort. If you had had any sense you would have put your confounded Expo under the guidance of the Duke of Edinburgh; no prince would have dared to bilk and rook the country as your politicians did, for he would have known that it might cost him his head. Expo! —" And then Sir John used some genial indecencies which I shall not repeat.

"But Sir John," I protested, "This is a democratic age."

"Democracy, sir, has its limitations, like all political theories," said he, and I remembered that I was talking, after all, to a great Conservative and a titled Canadian. But now, if ever, was the time to come to the point.

"We have hopes that our mighty effort may reflect itself in the future development of our country," said I. "Because you have been so kind as to make yourself palpable to me I am going to ask a very serious question. Sir

John, may I enquire what you see in store for Canada, the land which you brought into being, the land which reveres your memory, the land in which your ashes lie and your mighty example is still an inspiration? May I ask what the second century of our Confederation will bring?''

''You may ask, sir,'' said Sir John; ''but it won't signify, you know. I see, Doctor, that I must give you a peep into the nature of the realm of which I am now a part. It is a world of peace, and every man's idea of peace is his own. Consider the life I led: it was one long vexation. It was an obstacle race in which my rivals were people like that tendentious, obstructive ass Brown, that rancorous, dissident ruffian Cartier, even such muttonheaded fellows as Tupper and Mowat. It was a world in which I would be interrupted in the task of writing a flattering letter to an uncomprehending Queen in order to choke off some Member of Parliament who wanted one of his constituents appointed to the post of a lighthouse-keeper. It was a life in which my every generous motive was construed as political artfulness, and my frailties were inflated into examples to scare the children of the Grits. It was, doctor, the life of a yellow dog. Now — what would peace be to such a man as I was? Freedom, Doctor; freedom from such cares as those; freedom to observe the comedy and tragedy of life without having to take a hand in it. Freedom to do as I please without regard for consequences.''

During this long speech Sir John had finished the final bottle of his dozen of sherry. Those which he had drunk before had all floated, each as it was emptied, to the sideboard, where they now stood in a cluster. He picked up the twelfth bottle, and whirled it round his head like an Indian club, closing one eye to take more careful aim.

''You ask about the future of Canada, my dear sir?'' he shouted. ''Understandably you want to tell the world what I know it to be. But you can't, my dear Doctor, because I haven't taken the trouble to look. And the reason for that, my dear sir, is that I DO NOT GIVE A DAMN!''

And as he uttered these fearful words the Father of My Country hurled that last sherry bottle at the eleven on the sideboard. There was a tremendous smash, the gaslight went out, and I lost consciousness.'

How much later it was I cannot tell, but when I was myself again I was walking around the quad, somewhat dazed but strangely elated. For, although I had been baulked in my wish to learn something of the future in this world, had I not been admitted to a precious, soothing, heartlifting secret about the next? To be a Canadian, yet not to have to give a damn—was it not glorious?

And to have eaten the Charlottetown banquet in such company! A smile rose to my lips, and with it the ghost of a hiccup.

The Prophetess

Francis Owen

John Metcalf has a lot of evidence for his assertion that virtually nothing (and I'm not sure he usually includes the polite "virtually") published in Canada before 1945 is worth reading. The following story would seem to fit into his generalization. It is so overwritten in some places that you cringe a bit as you read it. Consider the garble of images in

> The wind increased and poured its vials of wrath upon the devouring flames, sending long fiery streams and serpentine coils hundreds of feet into the air, ever reaching forward towards the town as if eager to try its uncurbed strength upon the unprotected wooden structures that lay clustered in a heap.

Entire creative writing lessons have been devoted to less.

If it is so overwritten, why is it in the collection? Because its merits outweigh its obvious flaws. It presents a rare (and brief) glimpse of Vancouver in 1876, the year of the Great Fire. It is a vivid portrayal of the damage white settlers were doing to native cultures, and is remarkably sensitive to the issues of native rights and the environment, given that it was published in 1907.

My friend Weston and I were among the first to hear the call of the Golden West and to trust our future in the hands of the guardian spirit. Those were the days of the pioneer, the real pioneer, not the settler of today who is rushed at the speed of thirty miles an hour through the rocky solitude of the Superior District, on over the boundless prairies, "the gardens of the desert," and then again through the serried rolls of snow-capped mountains, by the brink of yawning chasms, beneath frowning bluffs and over winding rivers to the wave-washed shore of the Pacific Coast. Travelling is a pleasure now-a-days — no long, weary walks, no jolting over stony roads, no camping among the lonely mountains with the cries of coyotes and hungry wolves ringing in your ears.

At the time of which I speak the C.P.R. was in the process of construction and, in spite of almost insur-mountable difficulties, had hewed its way through countless walls of rock, until finally, arrived at Port Moody, it only remained to lay the foundations of its Western Terminal, Vancouver, the present Queen City of the West, but which then had only a few thousand inhabitants — daring adventurers who had braved the perils of an unknown land to carry the standard of West-ern civilization to the barren regions of the Pacific Coast. The bulk of the city clustered around Cordova and Water streets, stretching out on one side towards Hastings' saw-mill and on the other as far as any speculator wished to go, which was not very far. Back of this section to False Creek, where now stand hundreds of smiling homes and pretty lawns, was bush and brush, a tangled mess of fallen trees that crossed each other in hopeless intricacy, partially charred and checkered by fires, which had raged and laid low the monarchs of the forest, but leaving a horde of smaller trees which looked like a sea of needles, with thin sharp points rising high in the air, and their weird, leafless branches protruding like thorns from their sides. Large gangs of workmen were employed by C.P.R. clearing this land and making ready for the laying of a roadbed to the waterfront.

Weston and I had been attracted by the high wages offered by the Company to surveyors, and we had followed the progress of the line nearly all the way through the mountains. At this particular time we were in Vancouver and were quartered in a three-storey wooden structure on Alexander Street, which we made our base of supplies for the extensive journeys we were often compelled to make. The weather had been hot and dry, scorching hot; we felt ourselves shrinking perceptibly every day, and our health began to be impaired. As we had been working steady for several months without a rest, Weston proposed one day that we go for a few weeks' shooting in the mountains, adding by way of further inducement that we might run across a good gold proposition in our ramblings. For three weeks we fished, hunted, and prospected along the Fraser River, thoroughly enjoying the bracing mountain atmosphere and the beautiful scenery of the Canadian Alps. But the lonely life at last began to tell upon our spirits. Not a living soul but Indians had crossed our paths during all this time, and we began to long for the joys of companionship.

It was on a Saturday night, I remember it as distinctly as if it were yesterday, and we had decided to go down the river the following day on our homeward journey. We had gone for a last excursion among the mountains about two miles away from our camp. The sun was just setting; a crimson glow suffused the sky; the twilight blushed; the silver gems of the snow-capped peaks became golden with the sunset flush; the rushing streams seemed to allay their headlong course to be caressed by the lingering sunbeams, which left a purple hue upon the dancing waters, turning them into streams of gold; the birds spread out their wings to catch the radiance of the setting sun and warbled their evening songs of happiness and peace.

We were standing beside a clump of stunted trees which had climbed as far up the mountain side as their small strength would allow and had been forced to stop half way, whence they could see below them the sturdy heads of their stronger brethren, and far above the dwarfed statures of smaller but more daring and hardier adventurers who had scaled the slope even to the snow-line, but there had stopped, repulsed by the cool reception of the aerial spirits. We stood gazing at the glory of the sunset, lost for the moment in the grandeur and nobility of the eternal, fascinated by the varied shades of colour, and the succession of changes from silver through all the mutations of gold and crimson to a deep purple hue as if the blood of battling spirits had stained the sky. Suddenly an apparition darted from behind the trees, sprang upon a projecting rock, raised a skinny arm and pointed towards the setting sun. It was the form of a woman. Her face was wild and haggard and her Indian features tanned still swarthier by exposure to the sun. Large coal-black masses of tangled hair fell over her naked shoulders. Her eyes were weird and roaming, and flashed at times like diamonds in the night. Her only covering was a garment of leaves intertwined so as to cover her emaciated form and angular body. Tall and commanding in appearance, she rose to her full height, threw back the matted locks from her wrinkled brow, and with one hand still indicating the sea of fire in the West, she slowly raised the other arm and with a look of inextinguishable hatred pointed in the direction of Vancouver. With extended arms and trembling body, in piercing tones that penetrated the very stones in the intensity of their passion, she hurled forth her denunciation: "Woe to the vile intruders! woe to the impious city! The fires of wrath shall descend upon their guilty heads. They shall flee before my anger, they shall hide and cover when I spurn them with my vengeance!

"See these valleys and these mountains," continued the forboding spectre, comprising with one sweep of her extended arms the whole district around her, "they were the home of my people, the hunting ground of my tribe; the land of the red man. They lived and laughed; they basked in the sun; they hunted and they fished; they died in the land of their fathers. But the vile intruder came. He came with his internal devils that scared the fish from the rivers, that shivered the hills to fragments, that filled the mountain streams and hewed down our sacred trees. They drove us before them like sheep and we starved among the rocks."

She ceased, buried her face in her bony hands, and wept bitterly. Then as if her grief inspired her with renewed hatred, "Look at me," she screamed. "Look at my withered face, my skinny arms and emaciated form. Once I was fair, once I was beautiful, once I was loved. The idol of my people. I lived like a Queen. I was the Queen of the mountains, the mistress of the valleys; the fish came at my call and the birds obeyed my voice. That was before the white fiends came and disturbed our solitudes with their unholy noises and their fire devils. Woe to the vile invaders! Woe to the unholy city!"

With these last words, uttered in a perfect crescendo of emotion, she pointed once more to the ground, muttering to herself: "Three weeks! three weeks!" The ghostly phantom vanished behind the trees with a dismal howl.

As soon as we could recover from our astonishment we darted behind the bushes to see where she had gone, but there was no trace of the strange creature to be seen. She had vanished as quickly as she had come.

Silently we proceeded towards our camp, as the darkness was falling fast. Weston was the first to speak. "I wonder what she meant," he said. "I don't think I am superstitious, but—I've heard of strange things happening sometimes."

"Oh, nonsense!" I replied, "she is only a poor, crazy Indian. There are lots of them around. Something has turned her brain."

"I suppose you're right," he said, but did not look satisfied.

When we reached our camp we lit a cheerful fire, had some supper, and then sat down beside the blaze to enjoy a smoke. Under the soothing influence of my pipe and the ruddy glow of the fire, my thoughts went back to my distant home. Familiar scenes flashed through my mind; old friends and loved ones peered at me from the mazy wreaths of smoke. I was startled from my reverie by Weston's voice: "I say," he said, "haven't you heard that the Indians place a great deal of confidence in these wild women? They believe them to be inspired, to have the gift of prophecy, oracles in fact?"

"Still thinking of that," I replied impatiently. "I don't believe any of that rot. There never was anything in it and never will be. How can a poor, crazy woman know what's going to happen?"

"Well," said Weston slowly, "I'm not saying that she

does know or that she can do anything, but you know
that many people claim to have intimations of the future.
'Coming events cast their shadow before them' is an old
saying, you know.''

''Yes,'' I replied, ''it is old, that's the trouble with it.
It's too old.''

''Perhaps,'' was all the answer he made.

I dismissed the matter from my mind and supposed
he did the same, for he didn't mention it again. We
turned in for the night, and slept the sleep of the mountain climber.

The next morning we packed up and started for town,
glad to get back again, even though it meant hard work
and long hours. We arrived at Vancouver without any
further adventures and found everything in motion. All
was hurry and bustle. The work of clearing the land had
proceeded rapidly in our absence and scores of huge
piles of logs and rubbish lay waiting for the match.

It was Saturday night again, just three weeks after our
unearthly visitor of the mountains. I had noticed that
Weston had been very quiet all that day, but the reason
for it had never entered my head. I left him for the night
about ten o'clock in the evening and went to my room. I
tried to sleep but could not; all sorts of things came crowd-
ing on my brain. I rolled over and over; I tried every
possible expedient to induce the god of sleep to close my
eyes, but it was of no avail. Finally I got up, and, knowing
that Weston often sat up late at night reading, I crept
softly down the hall to his room, opened the door, and
peeped in. There he was, sitting beside the table, his
elbows resting on the edge, and his head supported by
his hands. A book lay near him which he had evidently
been reading. He did not hear me open the door.

"Hello!" I said.

He never moved. I approached him noiselessly and gently touched him on the shoulder.

"Good heavens," he cried, springing up with a terrified expression on his face.

"What's the matter?" I asked.

"Oh, it's you!" he exclaimed. "I thought you were asleep."

"And I thought you were," I replied. "What, what on earth is the matter with you?"

"The prophetess," he whispered hoarsely. "It is three weeks today. Did you not notice the sunset tonight? It was as red as blood. The sky seemed to be on fire. She was there. I saw her."

"Come! come! what nonsense!" I exclaimed. "Are you going to let a little thing like that keep you awake?"

"Why couldn't you sleep?" he asked, turning round sharply.

"I don't know, the heat perhaps."

"I do," he answered as he sat down and motioned me to do the same.

"I'll tell you what," he continued after a moment's silence. "I'm going to pack my few things tonight so that if anything should happen . . ."

"You're a fool," I snapped.

"Perhaps I am," he replied calmly. "I hope I am in this case, but I'd rather be a living fool than a dead sage."

"Why," I cried, "that blessed old Indian has forgotten the whole affair by this time!"

"After we came back to town," Weston rejoined, as he began to pack his things in a small trunk, "I made inquiries about the woman among the Indians. They were very reticent, but I finally learned that she had been a noted personage among the tribes of this district, but owing to an unfortunate alliance she had had with a white trapper who had treated her harshly and then deserted her, she had ever since dwelt alone among the mountains. Her mind became unhinged, and her people regard her with awe and veneration." He had by this time finished packing. "There," he said, "I hope you are right, but I couldn't sleep until I had done that."

I was awakened the next morning by a loud shouting on the street. Wondering what was the matter, I arose, looked at my watch, and found to my surprise that it was eleven o'clock. I opened the window and looked out. A fearful sight met my eyes. People were hurrying and running in all directions with spades, shovels, axes, and buckets. A huge roll of fire was advancing upon the little town, driven on by a strong west wind. An indefinable dread thrilled me. "The prophetess," unconsciously escaped my lips. I hurried out to the scene of the fire and found that the men had been ordered early in the morning to set fire to the large piles of rubbish. No one had thought there was any danger. All at once a strong wind had arisen, had fanned the flames of fury and whirled them from one pile to another, closer and closer to the outlying houses. The wind increased and poured its vials of wrath upon the devouring flames, sending long fiery streams and serpentine coils hundreds of feet into the air, ever reaching forward towards the town as if eager to try its uncurbed strength upon the unprotected wooden structures that lay clustered in a heap. Dense volumes of burning smoke obscured the sun and fired the heavens. On swept the seething mass towards the city in eddies and whirls that looked like a sea of serpents twisting and twining their coils around each other. Frail houses disappeared in the twinkling of an eye. A fierce crackling, a cloud of smoke, and then the fiery demons passed on, leaving the charred ruins behind to mark their path. The frantic people fled from the houses in every direction, crazed with fear yet fascinated by the aweful spectacle of destruction.

The fire had eaten its way to the waterfront when suddenly the wind veered to the northeast and the whole cloud of fire started on its path of annihilation in a new direction. Down Alexander Street it rushed, licking up the rows of houses as if they had been paper. I thought of my few possessions in my room, but it was too late to save them. I found Weston standing in speechless terror, pointing with trembling hand to the roof of the house.

''The prophetess,'' he finally gasped.

There was the wild woman of the mountains, with her long black hair streaming in the wind, her tall form reflecting the glow of the approaching flames, her weird eyes gleaming like burning balls, waving her long arms in wild gesticulation at the fire, her body swaying to and fro as if keeping time to the withering advance of the snake-like tongues of blood, and mute as her native mountains. Instinctively I started for the house to save the poor creature from a fearful death, but Weston seized my arm.

''Too late,'' he whispered hoarsely, and pointed to the rolling flames which were rushing upon the house in a perfect maelstrom. I looked again at the woman. Once more she had extended her long arms, one towards the west and the other towards the burning city.

''Woe to the vile invaders! Woe to the impious city!''

she shrieked in a voice that was heard above the roar and crackling of the blaze, and then the sea of fire received her in its coils.

"The prophetess!" cried Weston, and fell to the ground in a death-like swoon.

Under the Elms

Gail Herbert

At the *second* Waterloo Mystery Writers' Conference (and apparently the last), Elaine Driedger took me aside and said I should be sure to read some of the stories her friend, Gail Herbert, had brought with her. Gail, she assured me, was very talented.

I am a sceptical person. Everyone has high opinions of the abilities of their friends, their judgement coloured by affection and loyalty. My scepticism was wasted; Gail's stories, more concrete than Elaine's but no less complex, were beautifully crafted.

"Under the Elms" is not quite typical of her writing, for it is driven more by plot than by characterization. Mark and Rachel are two standard-issue people trying to cope with a world that has suddenly turned on them with a vengeance. Probably the scariest story in this collection, it should have you turning the pages very quickly indeed.

"It's so quiet here," Rachel Harris told her husband for the third time that day.

"You forgot the peaceful part," Mark teased. He hadn't been sure about building in the country. But now, seeing the dark shadows gone from beneath his wife's eyes for the first time in months, he felt it had all been worthwhile. Together they stood outside their new home in the hot August sun, avoiding the inevitable unpacking.

"It's not going to be easy at first," Mark warned. "I'll

have to keep working nights for a while to pay for the extras—like the landscaping."

Their eyes swept over the front yard, where their four-year-old daughter, Emma, clambered over a series of tree stumps at the edge of the property.

"Those will have to be pulled," Mark said, nodding in their direction.

Emma now stood triumphantly on top of one of the dead trunks, waving and shouting, "I'm the king of the castle . . ."

"Oh, I don't know, Mark. Why don't we leave them? If we had wanted a perfect lawn we should have bought one of those houses in that new subdivision—Woodlawn Something — you know, the one that sounded like a cemetery."

Mark laughed. "Woodlawn Acres. And it wasn't that bad—probably a lot cheaper in the long run." His face tightened at the thought.

"And a lot duller," Rachel argued, although she felt slightly guilty about having talked her husband out of the more reasonable choice.

It wasn't that she wanted a more expensive home. It was the land she desired. No . . . needed. She craved a space for herself and family away from the rest of the world. Not just a fence—she knew from experience how little protection that provided—but distance. In the city she had longed for entire fields surrounding her home. A clear view from her kitchen window, where anyone approaching could be spotted long before they reached her door. And it was perfect here. When the real estate agent had told her that a farmer, named Macdonald, had severed a lot from his acreage, she had jumped at the chance.

"They must have been killed by Dutch elm disease," Mark said.

"What?"

"Those trees that used to border the road."

"Yes, it's a shame," Rachel said, imagining their tall, leafy presence. "Think of all the shade and privacy they would have given us."

"I think we have enough privacy," Mark said, turning his head to take in the sweep of surrounding corn and hay fields. "It's not like we have anything to hide," he added, jokingly.

"No," Rachel said softly. "Just something to protect. Emma!" she suddenly called, beckoning the child to come. Then turning towards the house she said to her husband, "It's time we moved in."

Mark watched her go inside, marvelling at the depth of tenderness the sight of her thin, slightly bent shoulders could provoke in him.

The smell of her skin was on him everywhere. Mark stood naked in the shower, hesitating to wash away the sweet sandalwood scent of his wife. It had been so long since they had made love that the unfamiliarity of each other's bodies had brought about a fierce new abandon. He ached with the memory.

"I slept well," Rachel murmured as he returned to the bedroom.

"It must be the country air," he teased. They slowly smiled at each other, slightly shy, slightly in awe of last night's passion.

"I don't think I'll be able to get away until late this evening," he said. "Will you be all right here alone?"

"I've got tons of work to do," she reassured him. "I won't even have time to miss you."

"Good," he said, relieved. "Oh, do you think you could take some money over to the Macdonalds' today? I made several long-distance calls from their house. Don't worry, you'll like them."

"Okay," she agreed. "It would be nice to take Emma for a walk later."

"I just have to see if these curtains fit," Rachel told her daughter several hours later. "You play outside in the front where I can see you. I'll come and get you in a few minutes."

Through the window Rachel watched her daughter running over the rough ground towards the bushes and felt a stab of joy. "Please be happy here," she whispered. "Now where did I put those pins?"

After rooting through several boxes, Rachel returned to the window with her sewing kit. Out of habit, she scanned the yard. Emma was nowhere in sight. Rachel dropped the pins and raced out the front door.

Halfway across the yard she saw her daughter standing on the other side of the bushes at the edge of the road. She was petting a collie while an old man with a cane stood watching.

Rachel fought to control her anger as she approached them. How many times had she warned her child not to talk to strangers or go near unfamiliar dogs?

"Look, Mom," Emma said, innocently. "It's Lassie."

"Yes, she's lovely," Rachel answered, but her eyes were only on the owner.

She felt somewhat relieved at his age. He was probably in his seventies, with thick white hair swept back off a high, pale forehead. He wore an old grey suit that had once fit snugly on his large frame but now, with time and the sagging of flesh, had grown loose. Rachel searched his pallid, unsmiling face for a hint of friendliness or hostility, but could detect neither. Yet the pale blue eyes, clouded by milky white cataracts, did reveal some inner agitation. Looking into them, she felt, was like trying to peer through fog while stumbling over hazardous ground.

"I'm Rachel Harris," she offered. "And this is my daughter, Emma. We just moved in yesterday."

The man stared at her gravely. Then, awkwardly, he extended his hand as if he couldn't quite remember the simple ritual. Despite the heat, his fingers were unnaturally cool. "Lucan Moore," he said in a throaty voice.

"Do you live nearby?" she ventured.

"Half a mile up the road." His face remained expressionless, but his eyes never left hers. A question seemed to be forming in their smoky blue mists. Anxiously he took a deep breath, as if he were about to tell her something important but unpleasant. Then he glanced at Emma and changed his mind.

"Well . . . it was nice meeting you," Rachel said uncomfortably. She took Emma by the hand and led her away.

"Why were you talking to that man!" she admonished her daughter.

"I wasn't," Emma protested. "I was talking to the dog."

"All right, honey. Just stay in our yard from now on and don't go near the road."

"Okay. Now can we go to Old Macdonald's farm?"

Rachel laughed and hugged her daughter, determined

to put the incident from her mind. But as she went inside to get her purse she could still feel the unsettling gaze of Lucan Moore on her back.

As Rachel walked up the Macdonalds' laneway she couldn't help thinking what a perfect country scene lay before her. The century-old stone house with its white latticed gables sat squarely at the end of the drive. Bright red geraniums mixed with silver-leafed foliage bordered the old-fashioned verandah that ran the width of the house.

Leading Emma by the hand, Rachel walked up the wooden steps. But before she could knock, a short, stocky woman in her early sixties appeared at the door.

"Hello, Rachel!" the woman bellowed. "I'm Sarah and of course this must be Emma." She beamed at the child as she held open the door. "Come on in!"

"How did you know who we were?" Rachel asked, stepping into the cool, dark hall.

Sarah laughed, and her voice was warm and lively. "Your husband told me you'd drop by after you got settled."

"Oh, yes," Rachel said. "Here's what we owe you for the telephone calls."

Sarah thanked her and put the cash into her apron pocket without counting it. "Come sit down," she said, leading the way into a large, bright kitchen. "I was just putting the kettle on. Matt usually comes in from the barn about this time and he likes his tea no matter how hot the weather."

As if on cue, the back door opened and an elderly man in denim overalls stepped inside. The sweet scent of fresh hay mingled with the sharper smell of manure drifted in

with him. Rachel hoped Emma wouldn't embarrass her
by holding her nose, but her daughter was busy devouring the peach pie Sarah had set before her.

Sarah introduced everybody. The short, heavy-set
man grinned broadly as he crossed the floor to shake
their hands. Rachel's fingers looked almost as small as
her daughter's within his huge grasp.

"How do you do, Rachel," he boomed.

"Thank you for selling us the property," Rachel said.
"It means a lot to us to live in the country."

"My pa used to say nothing good ever came of living
in the city," Matt answered. "I've lived here all my life
and wouldn't want to be anywhere else."

Sarah brought their tea to the table and sat down
beside Matt. Rachel could see a distinct resemblance
between the couple—the wide, intelligent hazel eyes in
their bright, suntanned faces, framed by square haircuts
of the home-cut variety. She could easily picture Sarah
out in the fields haying with her husband, matching him
bale for bale.

"I was wondering why you decided to sell the land,"
she said.

"I needed the money for my old age," Matt said with
a wink.

"Be serious," Sarah chided. "You remember — one
twilight in the spring when that calf wandered into the
Elms and started to bawl. You had to go and get him and
when you came back you said you were going to get rid
of that strip of land."

"I'm selling some of my cattle, too," Matt told Rachel.
"I'm trying to make the whole operation smaller."

"You called it the Elms," Rachel said.

"It's always been called that," Sarah explained. "It

was always lovers' lane, too. Whether they were in buggies or cars, couples always went under those big trees to do their courting.'' Then she chuckled with a memory. ''When we were little kids we used to sneak up on them and scare them.''

''Until we got old enough to use it ourselves,'' Matt joked. He nudged his wife, causing a warm grin to appear on her face.

''I met another neighbour this morning,'' Rachel said. ''Lucan Moore.''

A look of surprise passed between the couple. ''Lucan?'' Matt asked. ''Down here?''

''He was on the road in front of my house,'' Rachel said. ''Why, what's wrong?''

''Oh, nothing,'' Sarah reassured her. ''It's just that he's kind of a hermit. Hardly ever leaves his house.''

''He never married?''

''Yes, when he was young. But it didn't last. We haven't seen Lucan down here for years, have we, Matt?''

But the old farmer did not answer. He was staring hard into his teacup as if he were trying to decipher a pattern in the milky brown liquid.

''The heat must have driven him out of his house,'' Sarah reasoned. ''They say it's the hottest summer in fifty years.''

Matthew suddenly raised his head and Rachel saw the pupils of his hazel eyes darken against the sunlight. ''Since 1938,'' he muttered, rising from the table. Without another word he left the house.

''Did I say something to upset him?'' Rachel asked.

''No, dear,'' Sarah replied. ''He's been acting strange lately. I think this heat's making everyone crazy.''

The light had begun to fade and Rachel finally had to put down the curtain she had been hemming. After supper she and Emma had gone outside hoping for a cool breeze. Rachel listened as the little girl chatted happily with her dolls. Emma was having a tea party, using one of the stumps as a table. Suddenly the child stopped. She was staring into the bushes at the edge of the road, her head nodding in agreement. Rachel came down off the porch and walked towards her daughter.

"What is it, Emma?" she called softly. "What do you see?"

"There's a man in the bushes."

A deep anger, stronger than fear, overtook Rachel. She ran past the stumps, tearing through the thick under-growth of vines and shrubs. She beat the bushes back with her bare hands but uncovered nothing. Reaching the road, she scanned the flat horizon. There was no one in sight.

"Emma," Rachel panted. "It's getting dark. Maybe you imagined you saw someone."

"No, Mommy," she insisted. "I saw him. He was hiding and he had a big stick. He told me to be quiet."

"He spoke to you?"

"No. He winked at me, like he was playing a trick on somebody. Then he put his finger over his lips — you know — the way you do when Daddy falls asleep on the couch."

Despite the heat, Rachel felt the prickly chill of having heard the unwelcome truth. But where was the man? There was no place to hide.

"What did he look like?" Rachel asked.

Emma lowered her head and would not answer.

"You said he had a stick. Was it a cane? Like the one the old man was carrying this morning?"

The child shook her head. Rachel took her daughter gently by the shoulders. "Was it Lucan Moore?" she whispered.

A puzzled look came into the little girl's eyes as if she were struggling with an idea beyond her grasp. Finally she said: "He wasn't old."

Rachel staggered under a wave of fear. She picked up Emma and forced herself to walk casually across the yard so as not to frighten the child. Once inside she locked the doors, then went from room to room, switching on all the lights until the house was a blazing bastion against the approaching darkness.

By the time she had bathed Emma and put her to bed, Rachel was convinced she had overreacted. Still, she knew she would never sleep until Mark came home. As she lay on her bed with her eyes wide open, the bright headlights of a car turning into the driveway flashed across the window. With great relief she sat up, anticipating the sound of her husband's key in the lock. But when nothing happened, she parted the bedroom curtains and peered out.

It was still light enough to discern the shape of a car, now with its lights dimmed, moving slowly across the front yard. Two heads bobbed in the front seat of an antique convertible. She watched in surprise as the vehicle came to a stop in the bushes near the edge of the road. Then a woman's tinkling laughter, as delicate as wind chimes in a subtle breeze, floated across the yard. It was an intimate, teasing sound that left Rachel embarrassed to be listening. But surely they knew they were on private property!

Then a flash of white off to the side caught Rachel's eye. Something was moving in the bushes behind the car. And suddenly Emma began to scream. Rachel raced up the stairs to find her daughter standing trance-like at her bedroom window. She clutched the child to her breast and carried her to the bed.

"Mommy, Mommy! Make him stop!" Emma wailed. Her eyes rolled back in her head. Rachel feared her daughter was having a convulsion. She rocked and soothed the child, who seemed caught in the grip of a devastating nightmare, until the tiny body finally stopped shaking.

"Was it a bad dream that scared you?" Rachel asked.

Emma shook her head and pointed to the window.

Rachel was afraid to go on, but she knew she must.

"What did you see outside?" she whispered.

"A car."

"Were there two people in the car?"

"Uh-huh."

"Was there someone else? Maybe someone watching them?"

"The man in the bushes."

"Was it the same man you saw earlier this evening?"

Emma nodded.

"What was he doing?"

The child began to tremble again. "He had a big stick and he was sneaking up on the people in the car."

"Maybe he was just trying to scare them."

"No." Emma said firmly. "He's mad at them."

"You stay here," Rachel said. "I'm going to see if they're still out there." She walked back to the window, bracing herself for whatever vision awaited. From Emma's upstairs room she could clearly see the entire front yard. But whoever had been there had vanished. The yard was dark and silent and empty.

Mark saw the lights on in the house and knew something was wrong. Rachel was a dedicated conserver of energy. He leaped from the car and ran to insert his key in the door, only to be stopped by the chain lock.

"Rachel!" he called desperately. A few moments later he saw his wife's strained face at the crack. She threw back the chain and fell into his arms.

"What's wrong, honey, what's wrong?" he asked as he half-carrired her to the living room couch. "Is Emma all right?"

"I think so." Then she told him about the car in the yard and the man in the bushes.

"But you never saw him?" Mark said.

"Not really." A shudder passed through her body. "Oh, Mark! What if he followed us here? What if he thinks I told the police? He swore he'd hurt our baby!"

They clung together, forced to recall that afternoon a year earlier. Rachel had been gardening in the backyard while Emma was napping. A man had scaled the fence and dragged her into the house. When Emma awoke to her mother's screams, the attacker had threatened the child's life if Rachel did not cooperate.

When Mark had arrived home he had found his battered wife in the bathroom washing herself meticulously, a ritual she continued to perform several times daily over the next few months. Every time he suggested they tell the police, Rachel would become hysterical. He knew it was the wrong decision, but he could not bear to make her suffer anymore. And when she had begged him to move to the country, he had gone along with it. Now something was pushing her over the edge, and he didn't want to lose her again.

"I think this man is Emma's way of telling us she feels insecure about the move," he reasoned.

"But what about the people in the car? I saw them and heard them . . ." Her voice trailed off. There had been something odd about the scene; something that she couldn't quite place. It was a detail that left her with the feeling that she was in no personal danger.

"Just to be safe," Mark said, "tomorrow I'm taking both of you to your mother's."

"No," she said, shocked by her own decision. "This is my home. I'm not going to run again. Just take Emma. Tell Mom I can't get any unpacking done with her around. Besides, the telephone is being installed in the morning. Then I'll be connected to the outside world."

It was another hot, airless day. The record-breaking drought was reaching a critical point for the local farmers. Rachel could taste the dust in her mouth as she walked across the yard. She was tracing the path of the car she had seen last night, searching for some physical proof that it had really been there. There were no tire tracks in the rough ground, but then the earth was very dry. As she drew closer to the stumps and the wild undergrowth near the edge of the road, she looked for broken bushes or crushed weeds that the weight of a car would surely have marked. But the area was completely undisturbed. She crouched beside one of the stumps and examined its surface, intrigued by the peculiar-looking growth at its base. From somewhere she recalled that fungi fed on dead trees, helping to break them down during the decaying process. This one was shaped like a woman's skirt, its pale folds flaring out from the dark- ened trunk. Not knowing why, she reached down and pulled away a chunk of rotten wood. It made a hollow, ripping noise and fell to pieces in her hand. In the gaping hole white maggot-like creatures scurried for shelter against the invading sunlight.

"Did you lose something?"

Startled, Rachel jumped up, then with relief saw Sarah Macdonald standing behind her.

"Just looking at these stumps," she answered. "Emma likes to play here."

"Where is your little girl?" Sarah said, glancing around the yard.

"She's visiting her grandmother."

"I thought you might like some fresh eggs," Sarah said, offering her a basket.

"Oh, thank you. Won't you come in for some coffee?"

After a quick tour of the house the two women settled in the kitchen.

"What you told me about the Elms yesterday got me curious," Rachel began. "I wondered if anything un- usual has ever happened here . . . perhaps a tragedy of some kind."

"Only the usual kind," Sarah laughed. "A few unwanted babies, some early marriages, maybe the breakup of others."

"But nothing . . . fatal?"

"Lord no! It was just lovers' lane. Why do you ask?"

"Now that I live here," Rachel explained, "I'd like to know the history of the place." Then she smiled. "Of course I wouldn't mind hearing the gossip, too."

"The story I remember the most was about Judith Moore. I guess because of Matt. He used to have a crush on her, too, before she married Lucan. Judith was a beautiful girl. Lucan was tall and handsome and had the biggest farm around. Matt didn't stand a chance. Of course that never stopped Judith from flirting with him. Or any other man, for that matter.''

''What happened?''

''Lucan and Judith were married for about a year when the rumours started. This fella came to work at the gas station out on the highway. Flashy dresser, fancy car. Everybody knew he and Judith were parking under the Elms every Tuesday night when Lucan was at council meetings.''

''Everybody knew?'' Rachel asked.

''Everybody except Lucan. Finally they ran off together. No one ever saw them again.''

''How did Lucan take it?''

''Real hard. Rarely left the farm, became a loner.'' Sarah shook her head in pity. ''It's sad how one thing like that can ruin a person's life.''

''Yes, it is,'' Rachel admitted, remembering how her own life had been drastically altered.

She heard it first—the low, rumbling motor of an old car coming up the dirt road. Then the flash of headlights blinded her for a second as the vehicle turned into the driveway. It seemed to Rachel that the fading sunlight had summoned her to the bedroom window just as the dimming of lights in a theatre signals the audience to take their seats. Now, as the performance began, she could see the two people — a dark-haired man and a golden-blonde woman—sitting in the front seat as the car crossed the yard, then bounced to a stop. Rachel listened. The same silvery laughter drifted through the air as fine and clear as music across a lake. The man and woman leaned intimately into each other until the dark outlines of their bodies formed a single shadow against the night.

Trapped in a powerful case of déjà vu, Rachel knowingly turned her eyes to the right. She saw him. He was crouched like a cat in the bushes behind the couple, wearing only a white singlet and dark pants. She knew at once he was not the man who had haunted her nightmares for the past year. But he was still a man to be feared. For as he came out of his crouch and moved stealthily towards the car, she saw he carried something in his hands. The "big stick" Emma had described was in fact a fence rail. Rachel's heart began to pound as the man reached the back bumper and started crawling up the trunk of the car. The couple in the front seat maintained their embrace, oblivious to the passion and rage poised in that outstretched arm above their heads.

Horrified, Rachel screeched out a warning. But none of the players veered from their roles. The club, silhouetted in the moonlight through the trees, came crashing down with a sickening whack. Rachel ran to the telephone and dialled the police.

"Send a car fast!" she screamed. "Someone's being killed in my yard—" Abruptly, she dropped the receiver, realizing what had been wrong with the vision both nights. The car had been parked under the elms — tall, leafy, living trees. The performance was over for another evening. Were she and Emma the only ones able to see the gruesome apparition? And how could she explain it to Mark? He'd think she was having another nervous breakdown and that this time she had influenced their daughter as well. Then she remembered someone else.

Matt was bent over a piece of equipment on a work

table. He looked up when she entered the barn, startled by her appearance. "Why, you look like you've seen a—" He froze.

"Ghost?" Rachel finished. "Actually I have."

Matthew smiled nervously. "I never heard of a new house being haunted."

"You know it's not the house, Matt," she answered. "It's the Elms, isn't it?"

She saw the old man's shoulders sag with an unbearable weight.

"I know why you sold the land," Rachel continued. "Two people were murdered there, and I think you know something about it."

Matt sighed. "Please believe that I never thought he'd kill them."

Rachel gasped. "You're the one who told Lucan!"

"She was making a fool of him!" Matt cried in defence.

"The way she made a fool out of you," Rachel said quietly. "Sarah told me how you felt about Judith."

The old man's eyes filled with tears. "It's hard to explain. She was so lovely. She had this laugh . . . like the high notes on a piano." He shook his head wearily.

"What happened, Matt?"

"It was the summer of '38. All the farmers were at the meeting that night. It had been hot and dry for weeks, just like now, and we were losing our crops. We'd elected Lucan to the council so he could try and get help for us. Tempers were pretty short, and Lucan and I got into an argument outside. I told him he couldn't even handle his wife let alone a political office. Then the rest of the story came out. Lucan stormed off looking like a crazy man. The next day he told everybody that they'd run off. But I always wondered."

"Did you ever tell anyone about your suspicions?"

"No. I guess I felt too guilty. Besides, it's a terrible thing to accuse someone of murder when you're not sure. And I wasn't. Not until last spring when I was looking for that calf." His voice trembled. "Then I saw what looked like the car with the bodies in it. They'd been hit over the head. It was awful. I knew it had to have been Lucan."

"But you never actually saw him?"

"No. But then, Lucan's not a ghost. He's still alive."

But how was that possible, Rachel wondered. She knew the man on the road and the man she and Emma had seen in the bushes had to be the same person.

Matt continued. "I thought somebody building a house at the Elms would wipe out all the memories. I knew I never wanted to see that scene again."

"Neither do I," Rachel agreed. "But how to stop it?"

"They say ghosts can't rest until they're buried properly," Matt said thoughtfully.

"Where do you think he buried them?" she asked, afraid of the answer.

"I don't think it was under the Elms," Matt said. "You see, he had to get rid of the car, too. The easiest thing would have been to drive the bodies down to his place."

Rachel shuddered at the thought. In her mind she kept picturing Emma at the window begging her to make him stop.

"Then we'll have to go there," she stated.

Matt's face looked tired and grim, but a spark of determination flickered in his hazel eyes when he spoke. "I'll get the truck."

The Moore farm appeared derelict. Broken machinery was strewn about the yard, left to rust wherever it had expired. The weather-beaten grey house with its boarded-up windows seemed ready to collapse. Matt and Rachel cautiously mounted the rotting stairs. Matt rapped on the door, and when no one answered, he shone the flashlight in the window. The old collie, barking inside, tried to hurl itself at the light in a feeble attempt at fierceness.

Tentatively, Matt opened the unlocked door, and he and Rachel stepped inside. With all pretence of guarding the premises gone, the dog whimpered with delight at the sight of the humans.

"Lucan!" Matt called as Rachel stroked the affection-seeking dog.

"Lucan!" the elderly man called louder. But only the hollow echo of his own voice disturbed the silence of the old house.

They proceeded down the tunnel-like hall where the entrance to the stairs and the main-floor rooms had been closed off.

On reaching the kitchen, Rachel knew at once that it was Lucan Moore's whole world. Within these four shabby walls the old man had spent most of his life. The room consisted of a wood stove, a single cot, and a table with two chairs. Against one wall yellowed newspapers were stacked to the ceiling—Lucan's only connection to the outside world. She was struck by the overpowering smell of dog feces and urine as she crossed the curling linoleum floor. Garbage from a ripped bag was strewn about the room as if the collie had been scavenging for food. There was no sign of the animal's master.

"Where would he be at this time of night?" Rachel wondered aloud.

Matt sighed. "I guess we better look around outside."

When they opened the door, the collie bounded out, yelping excitedly. In the moonlight they followed the flash of her white markings until she disappeared behind the barn. And then they heard the pitiful whining of an animal in distress. Matt and Rachel stumbled over the rough ground in the darkness towards the eerie noise.

Lucan Moore lay motionless on the ground, a shovel by his side. The dog was crying and nudging the dead man's face, urging him to respond.

Matt knelt over the body. "I'd guess he's been dead about a day."

"When I saw him on the road yesterday, he didn't look very well," Rachel replied.

Matt swung the light over the huge mound beside which Lucan had died.

"What is it?" Rachel whispered.

"A manure pile," Matt explained. "From back when Lucan raised cattle." Then his voice lowered. "I think we've found them."

Rachel shuddered as she recognized part of a car's grill that had been unearthed. She glanced back at the fish-belly white cataracts of Lucan's staring eyes, now understanding their message. He had wanted to warn her about the Elms, perhaps even make a confession, but he couldn't in front of Emma. By sundown he was dead, his spirit joining those of his victims in their gruesome drama.

Mark was waiting anxiously when she got home. "You had me worried sick!" he moaned, clasping her tightly. "I was just about to call the police."

Rachel regretfully pulled away from her husband's arms. "That's what I have to do right now," she said. Then she flashed him a brave smile full of hope and strength. "I have a crime to report."

The Angel

Robin Skelton

Robin Skelton has done an awful lot with his life, even if he was born in 1925. Poetry, teaching, publishing, witchcraft, criticism, translation, art . . . and short story writing. Skelton does not write nearly enough short stories, but it is probably a wonder that he finds the time to write any at all.

He is an expert in, to quote *The Canadian Encyclopedia*, "obscure Welsh lyric forms." He is also an expert in the occult, which explains the content of many of his short stories.

"The Angel" is a very whimsical angel indeed. It's not hard to imagine Skelton sitting by a fireplace, slightly sozzled, entertaining some close and even more sozzled friend with this one.

I met a chap once who thought that mice could fly. I don't mean that he confused bats with mice; he was quite clear about bats. He simply believed that mice could fly. He explained it to me very carefully one evening in the bar of the Horseman Hotel. He said that this was the way they got into his attic, and round the house, and he said that he saw them quite often perched up in his cherry tree, eating the cherries. It made him mad he said. His cat, he added, kept climbing the cherry tree but the mice were too swift for it.

There's no point in arguing with people who have beliefs like that. I guess there's not much use arguing with people about their beliefs at all. Another chap I know was convinced that his dog had learned to read.

He'd found him one day lying on the carpet with his nose pressed on an open book and his paws placed neatly on either side of it. "He has trouble turning the pages sometimes," he told me, "and he's pretty slow, but he's got through Mother Goose now and I'm trying him on something stronger." I can't remember what the something stronger was, but maybe it was *Travels with a Donkey*, or *The Kon-Tiki Expedition*, for a few weeks later the dog left home and was never heard of again.

I was telling this to a girl I met in the Horseman the other month, a nice girl with red hair and a proclivity for straight vodka — not a usual taste for girls I'd say, but I don't claim to be an authority — and she was quite amused. She said she had an aunt who had crazy beliefs too. She said her aunt thought that the paper boy was an angel. Well, that piqued my curiosity. I could have understood anyone thinking a paper boy was possessed of the devil — I'm not at all sure ours isn't — but angels are a different matter. I bought her another vodka on the rocks, and asked for details. "Well," she continued, sipping thoughtfully, "my aunt gets the evening, not the morning paper and quite often she's in the garden when the paper arrives. A year or so ago, the beginning of June it was, I think — she was messing about with the rose bushes when this paper boy arrived and instead of chucking the thing on the porch he gave it to her. He was a new paper boy, my aunt says, with blue eyes and blond hair and a sort of sad sweet smile, which might account for some of it. Anyway my aunt said thank you and glanced down at the headlines, where she swears she saw the words 'Ring Under Sofa.' Now, she had lost a rather valuable ring and had been worrying about it all day, and so she was startled. 'Good Heavens!' she said, and the paper boy said, 'You'd better believe it!' but not flippantly, quite seriously, my aunt says, and then he went off whistling 'Onward Christian Soldiers.' Well, my aunt went into the house, pushed the sofa to one side, and found the ring. When she picked up the paper again the headline read 'Riot in Sofia.' My aunt isn't really very superstitious—I mean she throws spilt salt over her left shoulder and doesn't put shoes on the table and things like that, but I wouldn't call her really superstitious at all, so she dismissed the whole thing as a trick of the mind." She took another sip of the vodka. "Yes?" I said.

"A couple of days later she was doing some weeding when the paper boy arrived and again he gave the paper into her hand. This time she didn't even glance at the headlines until she got into the house and had poured herself a cup of tea. When she did so she was so surprised she dropped the paper, and when she picked it up, the headline had changed again." "What was the headline?" I asked. The girl sipped her vodka, presumably for dramatic effect. "My aunt's name is Clare Parnell," she said, "and the headline read 'Clare Parnell Blessed.' When she had picked up the paper it read 'Air Personnel Unrest,' but my aunt was quite sure that she had not misread the words the first time. She has twenty-twenty vision and does a lot of needlework. Anyway she had hardly put down the paper when the phone rang and she answered it, and a man said, 'This is Radio XJV3,' or some such, 'and if you can answer the following question you will receive one hundred dollars. Are you ready for the question?' My aunt in something of a daze said, 'Yes,' more because she couldn't think of anything else to say than for any other reason, and the man said, 'What is the tune that we have been playing every hour on the hour between our broadcasts today?' and my aunt replied automatically, without any thought at all, 'The Saints Come Marching In' and she was right, and another man took down her address, and she decided she needed something stronger than tea and had a sherry.

"Two swallows don't make summer—or at least that's what my aunt says—so the following day she was out in the garden waiting for the paper boy and what might prove to be the third swallow at least half an hour before the usual time. When he did arrive she practically grabbed the paper from his hand and glanced down at the front page. 'Clare Parnell Impatient' it said, 'Bow Down Humbly.' My aunt says that, for the first time in forty years, she blushed and when she said thank you to the paper boy she did actually bow, just a little. She felt a fool she said, bowing to a paper boy, but then he might not be a paper boy at all so it was worth the embarrassment. Mrs. Tredgold from next door was also in her garden and when the bow was completed my aunt noticed her looking a little astonished, and gave her a straight look. Mrs. Tredgold said, without a trace of sarcasm, 'It *is* nice to get the paper, isn't it!' and my aunt nodded a bit brusquely. The paper boy was out of the gate by this time, and whistling 'Rock of Ages' which as no doubt you recall, opens with the supplication, 'Rock of Ages cleft for me, Let me hide myself in thee.' My aunt felt it was a little too appropriate to be comfortable, and wondered why there was no indication in the Bible that angels have a sense of humour. The headline, read again, said, 'Air Personnel Impatient. Slow Down Likely.'

"For the next two days my aunt did not venture into the garden during the afternoons, and simply picked the paper up off the porch. There were no further messages.

On the third day, however, and quite by accident—or so she says—she lost count of the time and happened to be attending to the weeds around the rhododendron when the paper boy arrived. He handed the paper to her with a flourish and said, 'I shan't be on this route again, I'm afraid. I've got another job.' My aunt was quite distressed. 'Why?' she said, gripping the paper intently. 'Oh, something came up in the classifieds,' he said, 'lots of opportunities there, you know,' and added, 'nice to have known you.' This time he left the garden whistling 'All Things Bright and Beautiful.' My aunt, carrying on the tune in her head, looked down at the headlines and read only 'Middle East Crisis Worsens.' Gloomily she stumped up the steps into the house humming to herself, 'All things great and small, all things wise and wonderful, the Lord God made them all.' It was only after she had boiled the kettle that she reflected upon the paper boy's words. They were, after all, the first connected statement he had ever made to her. What was it now? The classifieds — lots of opportunities — and then 'all creatures great and small.' Breathing a little harder she turned to the classifieds and the advertisement simply leapt out at her, 'Clare phone Dorothea Immediately Angel.' The only Dorothea my aunt knows is a rangy elderly female who is devoted to good works and dogs and is someone my aunt does her best to avoid. Nevertheless she went to the phone and made the call, and said she was calling in response to the advertisement. 'Well,' said Dorothea in her usual clipped accents, 'I never thought it would take an ad to make you call. Anyway you know what it is. Four weeks old. An absolute charmer. Nearly pedigree, and only a hundred.' 'What?' enquired my aunt, confused. 'The pup,' said

Dorothea, in patient tones, 'the last of the litter. Great companion. Don't tell me you can't afford it.' My aunt, of course, did not tell her that. She did not, for a moment, know what to tell her, and then, floating into her mind, came the words 'all creatures great and small' and the recollection that the hundred dollars from the radio station would pay for the pup quite exactly. 'All right,' she said, 'I'll call for it this evening.' When she put down the phone she looked unsuccessfully for the ad she had read, but did find a different one with Dorothea's telephone number attached under the heading DOGS FOR SALE. That evening, full of anticipation and excitement, she collected her new pet.

"It was perhaps a pity that she had not listened more carefully to the paper boy's whistling, for surely he must have held the note a little on 'great,' as the 'almost pedigree' pup turned out to be almost a Great Dane, or even (for it was curiously round about the head) almost a St. Bernard. As it grew, and it grew quickly, one might perhaps have called it almost a pony. Whatever its breed, however, its character was never in question. It was a romper, a leaper, an excavator, and before the next six months were out the garden looked more like Flanders Field than anything ever seen in Victoria before, and my aunt gave up roses entirely and concentrated on needlework. That dog is still with her, and a terror to all in the street." She emptied her glass and smiled demurely. "But your aunt still thinks the paper boy was an angel?" I said. She clinked the loose ice around in her glass. "Oh yes," she said, "she's convinced of it and you can't argue with her at all. Only now she says it was a fallen angel." I bought her another vodka.

O.R.3

Karen Wehrstein

Doubleday's party to launch Garfield Reeves-Stevens's *Nighteyes*
was held at the Tour of the Universe, a high-tech spaceship-to-
Jupiter ride at the base of Toronto's CN Tower.

As you would expect, the party was swarming with many of
Toronto's science fiction and fantasy writers. Karen Wehrstein was
one of the cluster of people who parked themselves at the same
Free Food table that I had started to become very attached to.

Baen Books, a U.S.-based publisher of fantasy and science fiction, has recently decided to publish her first novel, *The Sword of
Saint Mother*, which in Karen's soft, wry voice sounds like "The
Broad Fat Mother." (Why is it that the nastiest stories are written
by quiet, mild-looking, curly-haired women?)

Karen dreamed up this story while recovering in hospital from
minor surgery. I hope she never writes a story about editors.

"You aren't going to kill me, are you?"

Behind his mask the surgeon set his teeth.

The patient was middle-aged, gowned and wrapped
on the gurney, with a doughy face that kneaded when
she spoke, hair of a pale colour without a name, black
eyes that made him wonder if she had a secret psychiatric
history as well. Her stare was unnatural, always focussed
steadily on him. He couldn't remember her name.

"Say you aren't going to kill me."

Her problem was a simple one: a lump in her right
thyroid gland that a biopsy had shown had a one-in-four

chance of being malignant and therefore needed removing. A right subtotal thyroidectomy, a routine operation, called major surgery only because of the thyroid's proximity to some of the body's lifelines: the trachea, the carotid arteries, the spinal cord. In his career he'd done over a hundred of them. But some people were terrified of surgery instead of just nervous, same as flying in airplanes. This, it seemed, was an extreme case.

Both appointments he'd had with her had been peppered with the same words. Her voice didn't even express fear; it was unnaturally flat, a voice made of porcelain tile. It just kept repeating the same thing. Endlessly.

"Did you hear me, Doctor? You aren't going to kill me, are you?"

The surgical nurse was leaning over her gurney, saying what was always said to pre-op patients, whatever the degree of their nervousness, in a voice that brimmed with human kindness. "Don't worry, you'll be fine, you'll be fine, everything'll be fine." Even through the sterilizing agents in the air, the patient smelled the way the surgeon remembered from in his office: like an old damp library. Mouldy books. They'd put the warmed blanket over her as she was wheeled in through the green-tiled halls; a good policy East General Hospital had implemented, it made patients feel comfortable and secure, relaxed them. She'd been given a sedative, too. Neither seemed to be having any effect.

"You don't want to kill me."

They pushed her into the operating room, lifted her from the gurney to the table. The anaesthetist injected a partial dose of general into her intravenous drip. "Already given you some medication," the milk-of-human-kindness voice was saying. Yes, that's correct, he thought, I don't want to kill you. Most doctors are more interested in healing. Really. He wriggled his fingers in the skin-tight rubber gloves. His mask itched, and he couldn't scratch.

"Really, you don't want to kill me, Doctor."

Her oil-spot-in-pastry eyes drilled him. The flat voice was oily, too. Threatening. What does she have, he thought, a rich family who'll sue me for malpractice? They can be the Rockefellers, fine, I'm not worried. I'm not planning to kill her.

"If you kill me, you'll be sorry." The anaesthetist had pressed in the full dose. The nurses poised with the mask, hesitating. She's more than afraid, she's weird, he thought. We get them, we have to fix them. Yes, I would be sorry, he thought. You don't know how much. A memory touched him; he turned it away, as always.

He wished she'd been referred to some other surgeon.

"Tell me you won't kill me."

The nurse lowered the mask. "Just clean air, to clean out your lungs . . ." The two black eye-coals stayed on him, over its edge.

He had to warn all patients of the risks. "Putting aside the universal ones—haemorrhage, and infection," he'd told her in his office, "there's a chance the vocal nerve might get stretched, or the calcium glands damaged . . ." One never mentioned death except by an implication as slight as the risk; it just scared them, and didn't help anyone. She hadn't asked what the odds were, or even where in the above categories the risk of death lay. Just: "You aren't going to kill me, are you, Doctor?"

Chance might kill you, he wanted to say. Your condition might kill you. God or fate or whatever you want to call it might kill you. But dammit, woman, *I'm* not going to kill you.

It went against his grain, scraped like a scalpel up along his spine, because of that one-in-ten-thousand sliver of a chance. But he said it. "I'm not going to kill you."

The black eyes relaxed, and closed.

There was a mole on the crease of her neck where he'd planned to make the incision. He cut around it carefully. Aside from that it all went routinely, until he was stapling the incision closed. Then, without warning, for no reason, her heart stopped. It seemed as if the electrocardiogram machine had malfunctioned, which was what he thought until he felt her chest.

They did all they could, adrenaline into the heart, electroshock, cursing aloud, praying silently. Nothing remained, in the end, but to pronounce her dead.

He remembered the words of one of his professors. "We aren't God. We can't know or do everything. Sometimes we can do nothing. We claim power over disease because we and our patients find that reassuring, but sometimes disease is beyond our power.

"Sometimes patients die for no apparent reason. We put our technical names on it to hide our ignorance, but all the words 'heart failure' mean is that the heart failed. Medical science, where it is now, can't say why. Sometimes the flame of life just sputters out."

He was in bed, by candle-light, his wife, Ruth, caressing his chest, running her fingers through the hairs. She wasn't usually very romantic anymore. She wanted to make him forget it. He couldn't bring himself to be aroused; he felt sick. *Physician, heal thyself* . . . Maybe I should stop telling her when it happens, he thought. When it happens . . . as if it has happened more than three times. Four times, now.

This was by far the worst, and he knew why: because he'd told her "I won't kill you."

"But I *didn't* kill her!" he suddenly ranted at Ruth, as if she were the one he needed to argue with. "I don't know what the hell killed her, but it *wasn't* me!" He had the witnesses to prove he hadn't made any mistakes, if it came to a lawsuit. "I didn't say *'You won't die'*! I didn't promise her that! If that's what she heard, that's not *my* fault!"

Ruth looked at him with eyes that said, "Darling, you're a middle-aged man, a surgeon, a pillar of society. Get a hold of yourself." He took a deep breath, said, "I'm sorry, darling," and shut up.

You said you wouldn't kill me. You said you said you said you wouldn't kill me. The voice he'd thought was dead. In the darkness shone the bright lights of the operating room. He smelled the surgical cleanser, oxygen, old books. There were those eyes again. "Tell me you won't . . ."

The surgeon felt a sensation of falling into an abyss six inches deep, then sat upright, his body coated with sweat. Ruth shifted on her side of the bed, with a moan.

Nightmares. The outlets of repressed anguish. I wish she'd let me talk about it more, he thought. I could have got it out of my system, maybe even had a cry, so that wouldn't have happened. Now I'll never sleep, and I'm in O.R. again at nine o'clock . . .

He considered a sleeping pill, but decided to pep-talk himself into calm instead. Though he felt it was irrational, he found himself fearing the drug might trap him in his subconscious, subject him to nightmares without the option to awake.

He talked sense to himself, remembering again the prof's words and other good advice he'd had, but though hours passed his eyes wouldn't close. He observed Ruth's sleep patterns. He told himself he was resting, even if he wasn't sleeping. He'd had a little sleep anyway; that would have to do.

The patient at nine o'clock was like the morning sun through which he had sleepily driven, cheery and bright. She was in her late twenties, ran her own graphic design business, took judo, smiled all the time. In the corridor on her gurney, she cracked jokes with the anaesthetist, asked him how *he* was. She'd done her hair. When the nurse told her she'd be fine, she just shrugged.

Her problem was tonsils that were frequently inflamed; finally she was having them removed. This operation didn't even require an incision; once the patient was unconscious, he would work through the mouth. Even though she'd showered, under the watchful eyes of nurses, she smelled of perfume.

With the long curved scalpel he delicately cut through the root of the left tonsil. Then he felt something wrong. The shaft of the instrument in his hand moved the wrong way; and somehow, its appearance almost impossible to believe, there was a fountain of blood.

"The relation of the internal carotid with the tonsil should be especially remembered, as instances have occurred in which the artery has been wounded during the operation of scarifying the tonsil." *Gray's Anatomy*. As a snotty young medical student he'd wondered what kind of incompetent could do that.

Now he had not only cut the artery that supplied blood to her brain, but cut it severely. "Transfusion!" Hands rushed to aid, the silent panic of the surgical team translated into action.

The haemorrhaging was too fast, too plentiful. As his hands and theirs did all they could do, he was still a spectator, as chance, or God, or fate, bled her to death on his table.

When it was undoubtedly over he staggered out of the operating room, browning blood caked all over his greens. *A mistake. A slip of the scalpel.* He'd wanted a third cup of coffee this morning, but had held off, in case it made his hands shake.

Two in a row. Two routine operations, two minor operations. He thought of the young graphic artist, laughing with the anaesthetist. "Fine thanks, Doctor, how are *you*?" *She was hardly more than a girl.* He felt sick. He wanted to die. He wanted to cut his own throat with his scalpel.

It slipped in my hand. One moment worse than all the nightmares he'd ever had put together.

The chief surgeon of East General called him into his office. He sat down in the comfortable yellow armchair. He wanted to leap through the window, to feel the deserved slash of glass shards, to feel the just crunch of his body on the pavement six stories below. He watched his hands shake. Everything seemed unreal.

The chief surgeon was a kindly old man. "You look pale, John." He offered a sedative, which the surgeon refused. He offered a slug of whisky out of a hidden mickey in his desk, which the surgeon took.

He didn't ask what happened, even though the surgeon had been sure he would. He just said, "I heard about the thyroid case.

"I heard. That one threw you for a good loop. It happens. It doesn't cancel fifteen years of excellent work. Take a two-week holiday, John. Go south or something. Don't worry about your patients. I'll arrange someone to cover for you."

He and Ruth went to Florida. They walked along silken white sand beaches, swam with the painted fish over coral reefs, lay on lounge-chairs under the brilliant sun. As his tan darkened, the memory of two black days faded. He stopped reliving the fatal moment, the feel of the machine-scored shaft of the scalpel moving the wrong way, *wrong* way. Sleeping to the rustling of palm fronds and the distant roar of surf, he had no nightmares. They made love by moonlight that shone in the sky and danced on the water. On the flight home, bronze and rested and strong, he felt ready to face his work again.

The chief surgeon called him into the office again. "The tonsillectomy case — her parents are suing for malpractice."

He wasn't surprised. They were fairly wealthy, and they'd lost their daughter. "I'll settle out of court," he said. He knew his lawyer might counsel him to fight it, but he was decided. It had been malpractice, in the truest sense of the word. He'd screwed up and killed her. Why shouldn't he pay whatever they asked?

When he'd got malpractice insurance, he'd thought it was only for times when he was *unjustly* sued.

His premiums would go up, but he had enough to cover it; he'd just pull it out of their investments.

"You're okay now?" the chief surgeon asked him.

"Yeah, I'm fine."

"You're sure?" The old deep eyes leaned closer, as if for an examination.

"Florida was fantastic," he said. Despite everything, he found a smile in himself. "I think it was the cure."

"All right, good. Go ahead, then."

You said you said you said you said . . . The voice whispered in his dreams again. He drove it away with forceful memories of the beaches, the ocean, the bougainvillea sprouting scarlet all over Key West, and slept.

In the morning he felt fine, until he got to the scrub room. There his hands began to shake. Drugs were everywhere, easily available to him. A doctor's constant temptation, that he had never been tempted by before. No, he thought, I won't take anything. There's no reason why anything should go wrong with this operation.

It was a middle-aged man, with a tumour between his left third and fourth ribs, next to the sternum. A biopsy had shown it was benign, but the man had wanted to have it out anyway, just to be absolutely sure.

He didn't know anything else about the man. He didn't want to. This time he would strictly keep the doctor-patient distance. I need to be detached, he thought. After scrubbing he waited until the man was unconscious and draped, an anonymous body, before he went into the operating room.

There were the usual greetings. "Nice tan," said one of the nurses. But he felt they were watching him as he began, their eyes apprehensive. Understandable. Putting it out of mind, he made the incision.

Parting the layers of muscle all went normally, and there was the tumour, a greyish mass nesting between the two costal cartilages. Had it been cancerous, the sections of rib as well as some sternum along with all the other tissue in proximity to the mass would have needed to be removed as well, a debilitating measure; as it was he needed only to cut around the tumour's surface. *He's lucky,* he thought. Then the scalpel plunged three inches downward into the heart.

He ran, blinking through the blood that had spurted onto his face. He was afraid of what his hands would do. "You save him! You save him! I can't!" He dashed out the double doors, leaving a red hand-print on the glass, flew through the corridor screaming, spattering red drops on others who walked in greens or lay on gurneys.

His thoughts were chaos, a howling morass. As he drove careening through the city streets, avoiding cars, pedestrians, lamp-posts only by habit, one sensible thought came out of nowhere. *Gloves still on. Slippery on the steering wheel. Dangerous.* He didn't know where he was going until he came to his office, a five-minute walk from the hospital. *I must have gone the long way.* Patients in the waiting room . . . they were waiting to see one of the other doctors sharing his office, but it seemed as if they were all his. A plump middle-aged woman with bleary eyes. A young Latinate girl with tendrils of black hair. A black man with grey grizzle buried in a magazine. A mother with a toddler.

"Cancel everything! Cancel all mine!" he shrieked to the secretaries. They stared, hands frozen on the phone, over the keyboards. The patients blinked, eyes widening, as the greens, the mask, the blood, registered.

He stumbled into his office, tore his diplomas down from the walls, smashing glass, ripping parchment. "I quit! I quit!"

He fled their unbelieving faces. He drove without thinking. He had nowhere to go, no other skills. Home was out; he couldn't face Ruth. Where he wanted to go was death; but now he was on the highway, and the only way to die involved killing other people, and he'd done enough of that for today. The sun through his windshield seemed both unreal and ordinarily beautiful. He remembered a line from some book. "But one moment shattered all that." It occurred to him vaguely that his life had been shattered now, irreparably so. Inoperably so. Lives must always be shattered on perfectly ordinary days.

He found a cliff, on the Scarborough Bluffs, a three-hundred-foot sand cliff at the dead end of a road, overlooking the lake. He ran towards it, knowing he should just jump without looking. But he stopped short, going down in mud like a baseball player sliding into base. What if someone were down there, two lovers, some kids playing? What if it weren't sheer and didn't kill him, but just mangled him, and he woke up in some hospital bed?

He looked. The dizzying height wavered, toy waves lapping slowly on a flat beach, seagulls dipping on the steady lake-breeze below him. He thought of jumping, moved to do it, and found he was an ordinary man, with sane reactions; the back of his mouth went sour, sweat broke out hot and cold, his muscles locked and wouldn't move, and he knew he was too scared shitless to do it.

The car-phone rang.

"John? Where are you, John?" The chief surgeon. "Are you all right? Do you want to come back here on your own, or should I send people to come and get you?"

It was something to do, a direction. He drove back, on

his own. He thought of the psych ward. He'd be safe there. That was a sane plan of action. The sanest yet.

The phone rang again.

"Doctor Surgeon. Is that you?" A young, accented female voice. He didn't know it, but it sounded familiar. "I got cellular number from piece of paper, I am sorry." He placed the voice to a face, a dark half-oriental face under the sterile shower-cap orderlies wore. A Filipino woman. She pushed gurneys. "You must phone Manuel, five-five-five four-oh-six-seven. He know what's going on. He think you won't believe him, so he won't phone you. He know why your patients die. Five-five-five four-oh-six-seven. Please, you must phone."

He hung up, not knowing what else to do, and kept driving. He'd already peeled off his mask and gloves; now at another red light he took off his cap as well, feeling somehow that he ought to be as presentable as possible when he faced whatever music he'd have to face this time. He looked at the dashboard clock. Four hours had gone somewhere.

In the chief surgeon's office was Ruth, her rouge standing up like pink paint against her pallor; his lawyer; another doctor he didn't know but who had the impersonally sympathetic and penetrating look of a psychiatrist; a plain-dressed stylish man who glared at him seemingly with intent to kill, his arm around a middle-aged woman whose face was a purer expression of shock than he had ever seen; and two tall burly men in similar dark blue suits, who he knew to be cops even before they flashed their badges and introduced themselves as Metro Homicide Squad.

Ruth looked at him with eyes full of both fear and longing, as if to ask, "Are you really the man I know?"

The lawyer leaned and whispered in his ear, ''Temporary insanity is our best bet, John. Don't answer any questions, just say you can't until you've collected your thoughts. Just go along, we're with you.''

He turned to go with the cops. ''You dirty murdering son of a bitch!'' the man with the glare suddenly shrieked from behind, in some kind of European accent and the gravelly voice of someone who very rarely raised his voice. ''You murdered my sister's husband, you dirty motherfucking bastard!'' The woman sobbed.

He thought it was odd they should fingerprint him; no fingerprints would show up on the surgical implements, and several witnesses had seen who held them.

Ruth bailed him out; now the lawyer and the psychiatrist sat in his sunken living room and she served them all canapés. He gazed all around, at the colonial furniture, the smoked mirrors, the chandeliers. It was almost impossible to imagine he'd soon lose it all, had already lost it, in effect, after having built it all up over so many years.

He felt a sense of calm about it, or perhaps it was numbness; it felt like calm, though. What would be would be. It was only when thinking of the patients, or of the swearing brother-in-law or the sobbing widow, that emotion threatened to overwhelm him; so he blanked those thoughts out.

''You didn't know any of these people before, right? You're absolutely positive? So there's no motive that way.'' The lawyer was thinking aloud. ''Like a lot of other medical cases. No motive. But the press makes a big fuss of comparing them.''

The psychiatrist perked up when in answer to a question he mentioned the nightmares. ''Concerning the first patient? I see. And when you were operating on the second two, you got a sudden irresistible urge to—"

"No." He thought of the witness stand; he wouldn't lie there even to save himself.

"Well, what happened?" said the lawyer.

"I . . . I don't know, Al! It just felt like my hand slipped. Both times."

"Subconscious," said the shrink. "Perhaps an urge to punish yourself and subsequent patients."

"That doesn't make sense, John," said the lawyer. "You've been an excellent surgeon for fifteen years. Your hand couldn't just *slip*. Especially not that much. Even if you didn't sleep the night before."

"If you think I'm lying, Al, who in the world is going to believe me?"

The shrink ran him through a battery of psychiatric tests. All through the phone kept ringing, and Ruth fielded the calls. "Yes, he'll be pleased to hear that, thank you, thank you." Friends, associates, colleagues, calling to say they had faith in him, it had to be some mistake, they were behind him all the way. Not knowing how to answer except hollowly, he was glad to let her do it.

In the tests he came out as he would have expected to a month ago: intellectually oriented, perfectionist, overachieving, conscientious, and altogether normal and well adjusted. "*Temporary* insanity," the lawyer said. "Something drove you around the bend just before. There's witnesses, aren't there, that the first one was going on and on asking you not to kill her? That it got to you?"

It was the likeliest-sounding story, which, he knew, was all they wanted. Even Ruth, probably. He did not say that he'd felt no different before the second operation than he had any other operation just after he'd lost a patient, and that on the third one, if he had felt different, it was due to the two before.

Once is incidence, twice is coincidence, three times is enemy action. An old military saying from one of his profs. The homicide men were probably going by that to charge me, he thought.

"I'll get to work on it, John," the lawyer said as they rose to go, slapping him on the back. "Don't worry, we've got a good case here if we play it right."

Without knowing it, he had been dreading being left alone with Ruth. Now they faced each other, and stood for a minute that seemed like an hour.

"Well," she said, finally, "I'm sure they'll work it out and everything will be all right."

She didn't run to him, throw her arms around him, swear her undying love. He wasn't sure it was because she didn't want to, or because she sensed he didn't want her to. She was gentle with him, careful, as with a psychiatric patient, or a murderer.

Once . . . twice . . . three times . . . Enemy action. Enemy action.

At midnight, when she was sleeping, he crept to the phone in the family room. He had not memorized the number, but he remembered it.

"May I please speak to . . . Manuel?"

The voice was male and had the same accent as the woman's. "You the doctor? The one they arrest for murder? She said she call you. I don't think it help."

"Yes. She — whatever her name is — said you knew . . . something. Who are you?"

"Orderly at East General. It's not right. You no murderer. They wrong."

"I don't understand how you can know anything, but if you do, I want to hear it."

"You are — man of science. You won't believe."

"Try me. Please."

"There was . . . my uncle's house. In Philippines. Sometimes in there I get shivery feeling . . . like fear just on the skin instead of the guts, make me want to look over my shoulder a lot. Someone else there. Because there was ghost. I saw him once. He was see-through like mist, but shaped like man. He died in the house before.

"My uncle said when he get mad, he can move things around. Blow out candles, make the bead curtain wave.

"Now I get that shivery feeling from O.R.3. I don't want to bring patient in there now. That O.R. is haunted."

The surgeon sat empty-minded for a moment. He was tired, tired of everything seeming dream-like. He'd thought being arrested was the capper. No, *this* was the capper.

But he had to deal with it, rationally. Slowly, he formed words. "You're trying to tell me . . . that a *ghost* made my scalpel slip?"

"You don't believe me. I know. I didn't think you would. No such thing as ghosts. I'm sorry."

He groped for words, the phone clammy in his hand. The young voice was so earnest, so eager to help. "Look, it's not that I think you're lying . . . I've never seen one, but that doesn't mean I don't believe they could exist." He'd always held that position, without thinking about it much. "But . . . you're not even supposed to be able to touch them. They go through things." Here I am, he thought, having a serious discussion on the properties of ghosts. "How on earth could they *move* things?"

"I don't know," Manuel said, predictably. "Only God know. Pick them up with their spirit hands, I guess. But once . . . once the ghost in my uncle's house threw a knife across the kitchen. Stuck it right in the wall. In wood. Then when my aunt tried to grab it, it was moving in her hand, like someone pulling.

"You no murderer. That's all I know. I would say it in the court, but they'd put me up in Psych. You no murderer, and I said all I can say." A click, and a dial tone.

He sat stunned in the dark, remembering how his hand hadn't slipped; the *scalpel* had. *Three times. Enemy action.*

He phoned the number again. "Manuel? It's me again, please don't hang up. When did O.R.3 start being haunted?"

"I don't know, Doctor. A while. Maybe two weeks."

"Do you have any idea *whose* ghost it might be?"

"No, Doctor, sir, I have no idea. Lot of people die in O.R.s—ah . . . sorry."

The apology made the inward cringe that much easier to take.

"Do you remember how it started?"

"I got the bad feeling first time when I was pushing a bed with someone expired on it out of there. That crazy don't-kill-me lady."

I told you you'd be sorry, the porcelain-tile voice said in the dark, breathing mouldy books at him. *I told you I told you I told you . . .*

It all fell together. In his dreams; but even waking, it made no less sense, unlike most dreams.

With his astonishment came a certain peace. I knew it wasn't me. I thought it couldn't be me, it was impossible —and I was right. I shouldn't have doubted myself.

Ruth didn't even move when he dialled and spoke into the phone by the bed. He suspected she'd taken something. He couldn't blame her. "Manuel — thank you."

"That's no problem, Doctor. It was just not right, that's all."

"And . . . I guess we haven't really met, but . . . goodbye. I don't think you'll see me at East General again."

"No, I guess, Doc. Goodbye. And good luck. I pray for you in the court. I got to go, may I?" The bow to medical authority totally automatic, even now.

This is my way of reacting emotionally to the whole thing, he thought as he hung up, tears coating his cheeks.

In the morning, he imagined it. Him, now so thoroughly discredited, telling the hospital authorities, "O.R.3 needs exorcising." Where would one find a priest who'd do it, the Yellow Pages? He remembered reading an article in the (so very credible) Toronto *Sun* about a woman who accepted contracts to rid houses of ghosts. Her methodology: they were most often the product of sudden death, lingering out of resentment and inability to accept their fate. (That fit, he had to admit.) She would just talk sense to them, until they were persuaded to go on to whatever ghosts go on to. Sort of ghost psychotherapy, she said.

He could imagine himself on the witness stand. "Well, Your Honour, a ghost grabbed the scalpel." He would tell it as if he absolutely believed it—since he did—under oath, and insistently. They'd ask him how he knew, and then Manuel would get dragged into it; Manuel, who had only wanted to help, and had. They'd both end up in Psych.

Great, he thought. I've got the truth, and it's absolutely no good whatsoever, except to provide cold comfort.

He did go to the chief surgeon in the end. I'm already temporarily insane, he thought, why not? All he could think of was the other people who would have to enter the room, to be operated on, or to operate.

He wanted to broach it over the phone, to hide his face, if not his voice. But it seemed cowardly, so he made the appointment, drove to the hospital. He went in by a back entrance. There was a Toronto *Star* box there. "Surgeon charged with murder of patients," read the headline. It seemed incredible that yesterday morning he'd got up feeling bright and ready, that two mornings ago he'd been walking along a Florida beach.

The chief surgeon locked the office door and ordered his secretary to take messages. "How are you holding up, John?"

"All right, I guess. There's something I have to ask you. You're going to think this is very strange, and maybe that I'm insane, but morally I don't feel I have any choice."

The old man in his lab coat leaned closer, sympathetic. "Whatever it is, John, I'm listening."

"Ian . . . do you believe in ghosts?"

The chief surgeon blinked, and furrowed his grey brows, his posture straightening. ''Why?''

''Well, let's put it this way. There's something . . . amiss in O.R.3.''

The wrinkle-nested eyes suddenly became penetrating. ''John, have you talked to anyone else about anything of that nature?''

''No one that would matter,'' he answered. ''I know better than that.''

''You know if you said something like that to the press or anyone, it would just make you look worse in court. You realize that, don't you?''

''Yes, of course, they'd think I was permanently insane, not temporarily. I'm just hoping *you'll* believe me, in private. You've got to. Have I ever seemed dishonest, or flaky, or prone to gullibility?''

''No, you never have, John, and I fully intend to say that in court. But you don't have to tell me. Don't worry about O.R.3.''

He stared, in silence. The chief surgeon's face was a blank wall, letting slip no clues.

Not knowing what else to do, he pressed the point. ''There's something *there*, Ian. Something supernatural. And—'' He didn't want to say the word, it sounded so absolutist, so atavistic, but it was the truth. ''Evil.''

The age-thinned lips pursed, then said the words they looked unwilling to say. ''John, it's been taken care of.''

He heard and felt his hand, that had been raised to gesture, thump down lax onto the arm of the chair, bounce into his lap. He realized his mouth was open, and closed it.

The chief surgeon leaned forward and whispered, as if he had to, even surrounded by thick walls. ''You can't say anything about it, and neither can I. Or else I would, in court, for your sake; I wish I could. But it would just make us all look like nuts, or as if I were cooking up a crazy story to protect you.

"John, you're a good man. You're thinking of the other people who have to work there, and you've got a lot of guts to come here and warn me of it without knowing what I'd think. I admire you. Thank you." He sat back in his chair.

My mouth is open again, he thought absently and closed it once more. Too many questions wanted to burst out at once, and all were impossible to word. Break it down into the manageable, he told himself.

"It's been taken care of?" He heard a squeaking in his own normally deep voice. "The ghost?"

The old man suddenly leaned forward, pressed a thick gold-ringed hand on the surgeon's shoulder. "Look, John. You'll get off for temporary insanity, I'm sure of it. I'm doing everything I can to promote that, and so's everyone else. You'll have to do some kind of treatment, but it won't be forever, they'll pronounce you cured fairly soon. By then everything will be settled down, everyone will have forgotten about the whole thing. Move to another town, get into another hospital. I'll recommend you, and so will everyone else I can arrange to. Then you'll be fine.

"I can't do anything more for you. I wish I could, John. But I can't. That's all."

His temples were pounding. "It's been taken care of." Now his voice had caught a sudden edge. "The ghost." Anger. "You knew—why the hell didn't you tell me?"

"I didn't think you'd believe me, John."

His anger stopped short. Some part of him wanted to laugh.

"Yes, okay. I can see that, yes. How . . . How long did you know?"

The chief surgeon slapped his palm down flat on the desk. "All right, dammit, I'll tell you. You're right, you deserve to know.

"One of the nurses is . . . sensitive, do you know what I mean? She tips me off. I'm in contact with a woman in town who deals with ghosts. I don't know what she does, don't *want* to know what she does, but it works. I thought I could get her last week while you were down south, but she was out west, doing a hospital in Vancouver, and then it turns out she's booked up all this week at another hospital. You're *sure* you know no one will believe you if you repeat this?

"In the twenty-six years I've been running this unit, I've had to do this with the operating rooms five times, and twice in intensive care. I used to call a priest, the one my predecessor used and recommended to me, but this woman . . . her way is gentler, apparently, on the . . . spirits. She says it's some kind of ghost psychotherapy — God, I don't want to know. And she's better at not standing out, she just dresses up like an orderly.

"It's an aspect of patient care and community relations, John. To do it, *and* to cover it up. Who wants ghosts around hospitals? And who wants to *know* about them? But we get our share — more than our share. How can we help it?

"So don't worry, as I said. It's been taken care of. She started work last night.

"All right, John? And you know not to say anything

about this, for everyone's sake? I know you do, good, good, fine, good. Anything else I can help you with?''

To understand all is to forgive all . . .

He walked away from the hospital. It hurt to look back, when the rest of his life lay somewhere else, across the country in the quiet limits of a small town, perhaps, or in the anonymity of a large city. So he looked ahead. That night no nightmares came.

The Country Doctor

Marian Engel

I had the pleasure (as boring dinner speakers say) of copy editing Marian Engel's novel *Lunatic Villas*. It would have been a much larger pleasure had it not turned out to be her last novel, which casts a depressing cloud over the memory.

The most lasting impression of that editorial process is that we had to draw up a large map of the street the novel was set in, showing the second floor of each house, so that we could tell who could see into who else's bedroom windows.

"The Country Doctor" brings back fond memories of working on Marian's novel. It has the same liveliness; you can hear Marian's voice in it very clearly. I once read a critic complaining that Marian's characters are not quite real. The critic probably would have thought the same of Marian herself, for the characters sometimes seem to be pale shadows of her.

She had known she was going to enjoy this trip. There was no reason not to. She had had a busy winter and her ordinary life had seemed extraordinarily difficult, her voice rising every day to a higher pitch as she chivvied her son, Simon, through his duties, argued with editors, hurried through her work. Perhaps, she thought later, they had sent her away on purpose. Never mind, she was delighted to be here. Never in her life had she made so little fuss about finding a housekeeper for Simon, blocking out a series of interviews, dealing with photographers.

And indeed here everything had gone astonishingly well. She had liked the people she was made to see: they took her in like a long-lost friend. The town made her catch her breath. There was nothing else like it in Canada; early in the morning the sun sparkled on the granite wharves with a magical charm and innocence. She, who was most pleased when her eyes were pleased, revelled in it. The cynicism she had had to learn to protect herself from her imagination fell away: she walked naked of fear, light-headed, up the hill from the hotel to the party Tom Parsons was giving for her going away.

It was a funny party, and it got funnier as the evening grew old. They had started with mugs of tea flavoured with something Tom's father made in the back country; they went on to punch made of something Tom's wife Maureen's mother made in another part of the back country. It should have been nauseating but there was an astringency to it that also created a great thirst.

Most of the guests at the party were men. This was not, Maureen explained, a great place for baby-sitters. She sat by Diana, and once, when a joke was too broad for her taste, said, "Ah now, cut that out, Pete; Diana's here to write us up for her magazine and she'll think we're all bells and blisters." Diana had an impression that the expression was an edited version of something else. She started to giggle and had a hard time stopping. The others seethed into laughter with her. Then Maureen moved them all into the kitchen where there was a great round table loaded with pies and cakes. She made plain tea this time.

"Oh," gasped Diana, "I haven't had such a good time in ages."

"Don't they treat you well in the city, then?" one of the men asked.

"It's been such a foul winter that people who don't even believe in astrology say our stars are crossed: blizzards, strikes, floods, breakdowns: you know."

He nodded wisely. "Most of us are damned glad to be out of the rat race."

"So you should be," she said, catching onto the lingo a bit. There was a pause.

"You aren't married, then?" another one asked.

"Not any more."

"It's bad on your own, then?"

She avoided her questioner's eyes and stirred her tea rapidly. "Not so bad: you get your own way a bit more. But it's been an awful year."

"Oh, we have them here too," Maureen said briskly. "Give her another cup of tea, Tom. Now, tell us more about the great world. Do you think they'll switch over to the Tories there?"

Someone muttered about the fickleness of Hogtown. Diana shrugged. It wasn't the right time of night to talk politics, and the concerns of her Toronto friends were relatively meaningless here. "Oh well," she said as lightly as she could. "There are the ins and the outs, aren't there? And when things go bad you get the feeling you'd be better with the outs."

Tom clapped his hands loudly in her ear. "Well done," he shouted. "Ross, you should have known better than to ask her about politics but you can see she's been trained in a good school." The way he said it made her feel like a child or a toy.

Ross began to cough and sputter, and a man named

Kevin thumped him on the back. "Never takes a day off, that one," someone said. She looked up at Kevin. He had a long face and a long nose that cast a shadow on his upper lip, and flaming red hair. As he thumped at Ross he looked her straight in the eye.

Maureen was a big, good-looking woman. It must have been two in the morning but she looked as fresh as she had when she opened the door. Now she thrust the teapot over towards Ross and Kevin. Kevin stopped his thumping, produced a silver flask from his inside pocket, and handed it to Diana. "Put some of that in your tea to take the acid off."

"Now Kevin, she'll go home making remarks about boozing among the friendly natives," said Maureen.

Diana took a little, just a little, smelling it as she capped the flask and handed it back. It was Scotch.

Everyone watched her as she sipped from her cup.

"Now don't give her any more or she'll miss her plane," said Maureen, bustling among the cups.

Diana knew she should say she was going; the silence had set in that meant the party was over. But she was glassy-eyed, somehow rooted to her chair. She sighed, put her head on one hand, and said rather thickly, "You're all marvellous and I'm glad you've been good to me."

"I'm not only marvellous, I'm practical," said the red-headed man. "I'm going to take you home."

There was a strange kind of silence again. Diana looked at Maureen. "I'd be glad of the ride," she said, and winked, "if he's safe."

Maureen put her head to one side like a bird. Kevin stared at Maureen. Diana pretended not to see either of them. Kevin said slowly, "I'm safe as houses, dear."

One of the men, who was obviously drunk, put his head on the table and started to giggle. "Well then," Diana said as briskly as she could, "let's be off." She said her good-nights and promised to phone Tom and Maureen before her plane left. She walked down the wooden sidewalk leaning a bit on the red-headed man. "No offence meant," she said.

"No offence taken."

He put her into the car like an old-fashioned gentleman. As he fumbled for the ignition in the dark he said, "I like people to put their seat belts on." Then he leaned over, breathing an enormous waft of whisky at her, and pulled hers over her like a long, flat snake. As they drove down the hill, he said, "So you think you've seen everything here in a week?"

"Of course not. They allow me a week, that's all. And I have to get back to my boy."

"Is he a good boy, then?" The car purred like velvet under his voice. It was a heavy voice, but a courteous, educated one.

"No more than most boys. Sometimes. I don't know . . ."

"They're not easy to bring up alone."

"You can say that again."

"Are you getting the eight o'clock plane, then?"

"No, they said that one would be fogged, probably. I don't go till five."

"That's the better choice. If you've got a moment, perhaps you'd come and see my place, then."

She was only half surprised. "No," she said firmly. "I'm far too tired."

"What I meant, Miss Diana, was my house: it's considered a show-place. And furthermore, it's right here."

"You may have to hold me up."

"I've done that to people before. I won't keep you long. Tom's a fine fellow but I don't approve of their country hooch; you never know what's in it." They went up two steps from the sidewalk and along another walk. She could tell they were near the harbour from the salt in the air. They went up shallow steps to a hollow wooden verandah. She made out a wide front door with coloured glass etched with flowers on either side of it. He fished an old skeleton key out of his pocket and opened the door. "I should know, I'm their doctor," and pointed to a brass plate beside it. "Kevin Morrison, M.D."

The light in Maureen's kitchen had been dim. She realized she hadn't had a good look at him. The light here was no better. She sensed him beside her, big, stiff, giving off heat and whisky. "I don't usually meet doctors socially," she said, "or else they say they're something else."

"You can't hide what you are here."

He moved cumbrously in front of her and stabbed at a mother-of-pearl light button. "Here we are."

She was at the foot of a wide mahogany staircase with curving bannisters and broad steps. On the landing there was a suit of armour and then the stairs branched into two directions. It was a very grand house indeed. "Oh," she breathed like a little girl.

"I wanted you to see it before you go. They call it Kevin's castle."

"It's beautiful. You live here all alone?"

"Since my wife has been gone. There's a woman comes to do for me. They tease me a bit about it but I don't mind. My mother and her mother put everything they had into it, and I don't want it changed." There was a taste of authority in his voice. It came from doctoring, she supposed. He took her by the hand and she let him. Lately, she thought, I've been running into men who don't know what they want.

He opened a door on the right and took her into a room: it was a Victorian parlour with tables with knobs, a marble fireplace, and two twisted love-seats, the back-to-back kind you see mostly in cartoons. Great swags of velvet at the windows. "Do you use it?"

"You're a practical woman. I like you. No." He led her through more doors into a dining room with crystal vinaigrettes on a big carved sideboard. "No, I mostly use my consulting rooms on the other side."

From the dining room they went into a pantry, then a vast kitchen where the only new things were a refrigerator and a glass vase of coffee simmering on an iron stove. He turned the stove off somehow, and reached into a cupboard. "Milk and sugar?"

"Black."

"Hard on the liver. And the tongue. Come on, I'll give you the rest of the grand tour and we'll come back."

The staircase creaked. He took her, as usual, to the right. "They were shipbuilders in the old days," he said. "They cared about carpentry. I don't know where they got the tin suit. She used to travel."

"Is she dead?"

"Oh, long gone. She wasn't much of a pleasure. People with taste are not, on the whole. But she cared."

She followed him up the staircase, dead with drink and fatigue, thinking, I've met so many men since I left Jack, and in another country there'd be portraits on these walls: that's what's funny, no portraits. "There are no portraits," she said, for something to say.

"That wasn't our style. I suppose there wasn't enough for pictures, or she got rid of them. There might be some in the box-room, if you'd care to look."

It's when I'm tired I'm whiny, she thought. She wanted to whine now. She said nothing, just followed him. "This was her spare room," he said, "if I recall," to a roomful of heavy furniture, quickly lighted and turned out. "And, this was Mama's." A grand, large, airy room complete to the pink flowered jug and basin on the wash stand, with a handsome canopied bed.

"Did your wife live here?"

"No, she wouldn't stay. It drove us apart. What would you think of it?"

"I'm not the domestic type," she muttered weakly.

"I thought not." He laughed, and took her hand firmly. "Oh," pulling some drapes aside at the galleried end of the stairs, "nobody is, these days. Can you see out there?"

Out over the harbour the dawn was coming up, rosy-fingered indeed. He moved towards her, closing the curtains again as he did so, and slid an arm around her. He was much taller than she was and she felt small and for a moment, just a moment, safe. Then she looked up at him and his very big, very white face and saw that it was crinkled and cracked with a thousand wrinkles, as if he had suddenly aged or cracked like the glaze on a jug; his mouth was a wide, red gash, and she was afraid of him. She thought, his hair's not natural, it's too red and too neat, like a piano-tuner's wig. I have to stop picking up men, there could be bodies in those big wardrobes. But it was too late to turn away and she let him kiss her. His skin was dry and harsh, but his mouth was soft and not too probing.

He resumed the tour as if nothing had happened. "There are a lot of little rooms over the kitchen," he said, "little bedrooms and box-rooms. And here's the one I like best."

It was a big cheerful room with a fireplace with carved marble faces and two velvet armchairs before it. She sank down in one and rubbed her cheek against its shoulder. "I'm tired, Kevin," she said, "too tired to think or to feel or to take in any more. I want to go home like a bad song."

"Give me your hand."

She was hesitant, but she knew her hands didn't come off like rubber gloves so she held one out. He pulled her to her feet with it and half led, half carried her to bed. She was going to protest, but her head touched the pillow and she fell asleep.

In the morning she woke, thinking, where am I, what have I done, my head, the red-headed man . . . She remembered words but no touch. She looked over to the other side of the bed; sure enough, it was untouched. She felt herself. She had all her clothes on but her jacket and boots: a gentleman. A man of honour. On the night table beside her was a piece of paper, a glass of water, two aspirins. "Back at ten," the piece of paper said. It was from a prescription pad.

She got up, full of guilt. I'm like him, I'll never get used to the new ways, she thought. Waking up in a strange bed, put there by a strange man; it's too much for me. Her mouth tasted like old, rotten clay and her head banged its brain against its bone. Hooch, she thought. Screech. Ouch. She gagged the water down. Then heaved herself out of bed and looked out the window. Sun glinted on the harbour. But not very high. It

was only seven by her watch once her eyes came in focus.
Well, she thought, at least he isn't here with me. I could
have sworn he would be. An odd man: an odd house.
Under the lamp, he looked like a puffball: touch him and
he'd fly away.

No matter who or what or without whom she'd been
with she felt dirty, soiled: a week rushing around intrud-
ing on people's lives, a week pretending she wasn't
there, barging in, leading them on, remembering. A
week without being herself. And now, instead of a motel
bed, a brass bed with an embossed cotton spread and a
note beside it. She tried to think what to do and decided
the worst thing here was to go back to the motel too
early: everyone is visible in the dawn. She went into the
bathroom next door and turned on the taps on the sphinx
of a tub. They gushed brown, then they cleared. They
were no worse than her, she decided, as she got in. The
towels were white, and the wash-cloths, and the bath
mat.

She got out, refreshed, and instead of her clothes (back
at ten, puffball or wig or not) she put on a pleated white
cotton night-shirt that hung on the back of the panelled
white enamelled door. Took her own clothes into the
bedroom, draped them as modestly as possible on the
near velvet chair and crawled back into bed. Slept.
Again. Good. So often she could not.

Woke again. Brilliant sun pouring in but something
between . . . what? A large face, white: big-featured. I
remember the mouth, she thought. She lay like a baby,
blinking, staring up. He bent towards her. A telephone
rang. He left.

What a big face, she thought, broad in the cheeks,
wide-mouthed. Something about the eyes. I don't know

what. Red hair, still. Not so much a kind face as a blank one. The crinkles are gone. Must be a . . .

Her morning body was stirring now. She missed him. A little. She had only known him a little.

He came back. She was lying there, patient. She had remembered he was a doctor. ''There's been an accident in the woods,'' he said. ''I can't even take you to the motel. The ambulance is picking me up.'' He ran a finger along her lips. ''I'm sorry.''

''It's okay,'' she said, because, what else? She didn't know him. ''Take care of them, huh?''

''I will. If you want a taxi, call the Vets.''

''Okay, off you go.'' As if to Simon, or so many other men.

He was gone. She got out of bed and dressed and tried to make the bed as exquisitely as the other side of it indicated. She failed, but her effort was respectable. Then she turned and went to hang up the night-shirt. She was finishing her period and had left a spot. She looked around at the exquisite room and quickly, fur- tively, scrunched the night-shirt into a ball and put it in the bottom of her purse.

On the way downstairs, she looked at the house again. She saw it this time as a stage, a proscenium arch. The hall was grander than the rooms around it: they had started big and finished small. Of course there were no pictures.

Then she remembered that some time in the middle of the night she had seen herself as the mistress of this house, failing to dust its grand bannisters. Keeping Simon from scratching things. Stoking the stove, order- ing the retainer in the mob-cap about. It would be easier, she thought, to live without imagination.

She made sure the door was on the latch behind her and made her way down the bumpy street to the motel. Flounced onto her bed, read her notes again, organized her packing, made up her face again. Ran the powder over it with the odd feeling that it, too, would fly away. Remembered the red-haired man's face under the landing light, fractured by a fractured lampshade, vulnerable, powdered as a dusty miller's, old. Then his face in the morning, hanging over hers. Simon's, she thought.

Maureen called at noon. They had lunch in the coffee shop and there was time to put in till the evening plane. "Kevin took you home all right?"

"Sure, fine."

"He's a card, that Kevin."

"Is he?" Rather I should probe, she thought, than let Maureen.

"Oh, I was so mad at him letting on he was a bachelor and him with his wife and five kids and that museum of his where his office is."

"Museum?"

"His mother's house. The Pigott Museum. After her mother. It runs in the female line with them: the money, not the red hair. It's where his office is. Didn't he take you there? We all thought he would."

"I'm afraid I got out of the car and went right to sleep."

"Oh, he does that whenever he can pick up a woman, takes them back there and shows off the house and talks about his mother."

"Perhaps I ought to go up to the museum, then," she tried to fend Maureen off, "and put it in my article?"

"Oh, I wouldn't bother. It's just an old house, now. My daughter Eileen works there on the weekends. It's through her I know he takes women there. Poor Annie has her work cut out for her, looking after kids for the grand Dr. Morrison. He's a real pig, I tell you, a pig.''

"Honestly, Maureen, he left me off and I was too tired to notice. If he was Casanova himself, I would still have fallen dead asleep.'' Though inside herself something was merrily telling her stories about night-shirts.

"You've had a good time here, then?''

"I really have, and I'm grateful, Maureen." Her body stirring for something quite other. "And you and Tom made it possible." Not hypocritically: they did.

If she was very hungover, so was Maureen. They held their hands out on the table but lacked the coordination to make them meet. In the end, she went back to the counter and asked to extend her stay another day. The girl said, "If you're getting the five plane, no one else is coming, I can let you get away with it."

"Will you wake me up?''

"Sure. If you can sleep, love, you probably need it.''

But she could not sleep; her nerves were stretched and her temples still pounded with the hangover. She lay rigid as a bow on the bed and at last sprang up. "I'll at least find out the truth," she thought. She looked in the telephone directory and plunged out her door.

The motel was on the harbour; the museum was on the top street along the side of the hill that limited the growth of the town. The home address of Kevin Morrison was on a street parallel to both, a narrow street that looked as if it ought to be cobbled, so narrow the telephone lines were attached to the stone houses themselves, not on poles. The front doors of the houses were level with the sidewalk. In case they opened outwards she walked in the road.

Number seventeen had a bow-window, with a couple

of panes of bottle glass. In the window was a small, red-headed child and when she went past it pressed its belly against the window, squinted and stuck out its tongue malevolently. She turned and almost ran back to the motel.

"Oh, it's you." said the girl at the desk. "The five plane's been cancelled and Dr. Morrison will be around to pick you up for tea at half-four."

So that was that.

He looked more reliable in the last of the daylight. As if, this time, his long face would not threaten to slide off. "Hair of the dog," he said, "I think. We'll just go on up to the house."

Oh God, she thought, what story's he going to string me now. She began to demur.

"Nonsense," he said firmly. "You can't eat in that coffee shop again, old Mary's never heard of anything but frying in whale oil. And if you want to drink you'll have to go into the men's and it's no place for a lady." So they lurched up in his car.

This time he took her into his consulting rooms, which were large and shabby. There were two leather chairs and two great black rockers that were covered with something between imitation leather and horsehair. She remembered the stuff from her grandmother's house. It stuck to children's bare legs like adhesive tape. She sat down on one of the leather ones. He disappeared into what looked like an examining room and returned with whisky and glasses and ice. "Now," he said, "to the inevitable."

She thought of the red-headed child, the house on Whiteside Street. "What I can't make out," she said, "is, are you married or are you not?"

"I'm as married as you. Look, there's something you

didn't see last night I want to show you. Don't be afraid, I'm not Lothario. Come up the grand stairs again.''

They got to the top and went round to the front under the hanging light. ''Oh,'' he said, ''but first . . .'' and put his arms around her. She looked up at him curious to see if his face would again begin to disintegrate. She looked right into his eyes and saw nothing there but narrow pupils, a frightening intensity. She closed her eyes. She heard a harsh little bird-like voice saying ''You're just another one, just another one. One of the many, many, many. And he always begins here, right here. He's a bad, bad man and of that there's no doubt.''

''What's wrong?'' he whispered.

She shivered. ''Cold, I guess.''

''Never mind, I'll warm you. We'll go down now.''

Downstairs in the leather-chaired room she said, ''Look, I don't know anything about you. Maureen says you've family, you say you're on your own. . . . I don't like fouling another woman's nest.''

The telephone rang. He picked it up at once, looking away from her. Scribbled something on a pad. Sighed and stood up.

''I didn't think you were the sort to fuss,'' he said. ''I'm as free as you are, that's the truth of it. But not quite free enough. I've got to go. Mrs. Heaps has taken a turn, but it's not far. I won't be long. You can stay or go as you like. If you stay there's a ham in the pantry there to have a bit of. If you go . . . well, remember, I like you.''

He hitched up his trousers, straightened his tie, picked up his bag, and went out.

She decided to finish her drink and thought, at least I'll sleep tonight. She found an old *National Geographic* in the piles of magazines on the table and began to leaf through it and dozed off.

When she woke with a start, it was dark, and there was a creaking noise. She reached up as if she knew it was there and pulled the cord of an old-fashioned standard lamp. One of the black rocking chairs was creaking. She wondered if he'd come and gone and left it rocking, but when she got up to see it, there was neither dent nor warmth to the seat.

Outside, the wind had risen. She remembered the house was high on the hill. Somewhere a branch was groaning against a wall. Somewhere a shutter was flapping. Gingerly she stepped out into the great hall and listened. It was one of the front shutters, surely. He'd be pleased to find her there when he came back. She'd just fix the shutter and come down and have some of that ham.

At the top of the stairs she switched on the great lamp and stood and listened. There was no sound of the banging shutter now. Instead, as she moved under the lamp, the voice she had heard earlier, a bird-screeching malevolent voice, said, "He's gone, I told you, he always goes, he's better drowned, isn't he?" and began to cackle and laugh.

You don't have to be gullible to panic at a voice like that, she said to herself as she fled down the stairs. You don't have to believe in things that go bump in the night to be scared of them. She lit into the consulting room, scribbled on the pad by the phone "You are late, call me at motel, D.," grabbed her purse and skittered over the verandah to the street. Ham or no ham, she thought, I'm going to bed. Which she did.

Early, early in the morning the telephone shrieked at her. She answered groggily, hardly knowing where she was. "Kevin's gone," Maureen said. "Is he with you?"

"No," she said.

"I'm not collecting evidence, I have to know where he is."

"Not here. I haven't seen him since last night."

"What time last night?"

"About six."

"I'll be right over."

Oh God, she thought as she threw on her clothes, I get in these messes, why did I get involved? how the hell? . . . And Maureen was pounding on her door.

"You'll think me an idiot or a detective," she panted, "but I'm that scared. Old Mr. O'Connor was taken bad last night and they couldn't find him anywhere and it's the fifteenth of May and I've such a . . . Tell me what happened."

So she told how she had gone up to the house with him. "I wanted to get the story straight. You said he had a wife."

"Oh he did indeed once. And such a wife!"

"Is she gone?"

"She was a jealous little bitch, that one, and no better than she should be. Now tell me, you said he got a call . . . ?"

"About half past six, perhaps earlier. He said he wouldn't be long. A Mrs. Heaps."

Maureen turned white. "A Mrs. Heaps! What happened then?"

"I fell asleep. When I woke up it was dark. One of the rocking chairs was swaying and a shutter was banging. It was too spooky. I got out."

"You didn't go upstairs, then?"

"As a matter of fact I did . . . to try to find and latch the shutter."

"There's no shutters on that house, though there were on the other. Now, tell me, Diana, this is serious, see, nothing to do with you — you're both lonely why shouldn't you . . ."

"Annie and the children?"

"Annie's his sister, and keeps the house on Whiteside Street. She has two of her own as well. I think one's Tom's, the rapscallion, but that's neither here nor there. What did you hear, then, upstairs?" Maureen was leaning on the dresser, clenching her fists until her knuckles were white.

"Hear? hear? Well, the shutter stopped." Diana closed her eyes, then remembered. "Maureen, I could swear I heard a voice saying 'He always does it here. You're one of many. He's better drowned.'"

"My God," said Maureen, and began to dial again. "Tom, Tom, drag the pond," she said. Slammed the receiver down. Then she put her face in her hands and started to cry.

"I wish you'd tell me what all this is about," Diana said quietly.

"Oh, if I did, you'd only put it in your article."

"I certainly wouldn't. I've made a fool of myself."

"Look, I'm going out there now. I just hope you aren't right."

"Wouldn't Mrs. Heaps . . . ?"

"That was her name before she got her hands on him, the bitch. You get some breakfast now and I'll come back and tell you what's happened." Maureen stood up, taller now, and somehow older. They're all related, Diana thought.

Diana shook her head as if to get water out of her ears and went to the coffee shop. She felt as if everyone was staring at her. She waded through her ham and eggs as stolidly as she could. I must be crazy, she thought, or they must be. Announcements do not come from puffball lamps. Reality exists. Reality must exist. If it doesn't exist here it does at home and I hope I can get there soon.

She was on her second cup of weak coffee when Tom slid into the booth across from her. "He's gone," he said in a quiet voice.

"I don't understand."

"You wouldn't. It's a long old story. There's no Mrs. Heaps. That was her name when she lived there, out by the pond."

"He said it wasn't far, he wouldn't be long."

"He was a broken man."

"I didn't help him. I thought he might just be fooling around."

"She said it was him or her. In the end, it was both of them. They ate each other up, as if it was the poem, like."

"It's really beyond me."

"It's beyond all of us. Some things are. There's a plane laid on at ten."

"Was he in the pond?"

"Oh, in the pond all right."

"And his face?"

He gave her a long look, as if he was going to be sick. "You saw that too. You saw that too. And you never knew you were one of us before, did you?"

She turned away and began to cry.

In the hour before the bus was to leave for the airport she clambered up the hill and let herself into the museum of the house. Inside the door she grabbed an old blackthorn stick from a Chinese umbrella stand. She ran up the stairs, banging against the armour on the landing, not stopping to see what happened behind her. She ran along the top corridor to the front, to the great hanging lamp; she hit it a shattering blow. Glass flew around her and a cloud of old dust and dead moths flew out. The front hall was still afloat with moths and shards of glass as she banged the door behind her.

In the plane, she sucked her knuckles and whimpered for him.

A month later she was having dinner with Oliver Crown. "You've been there," he said, naming the town. "What's it like?"

"Oh, picturesque," she said evasively.

"I know that, love, I read your article. But there must be more to it than that."

"I don't know, Oliver, there's just people, like anywhere else."

"I've been asked to go there. Some rigamarole about a ghost in a pond."

"The Spook of Randal's Cove? Honestly, Oliver! You don't believe in stuff like that. You'd do much better," she said, modestly muddling in her fruit salad, "to stay here and marry me. Simon needs a father."

He looked at her long and hard. "Are you being straight?"

"Sort of," she said, playing with her fork, staring at the scar on her hand.

"It sounds," he said quietly, "like a good idea."

She sighed with relief.

CHIPS

Judith and Garfield Reeves-Stevens

This story sparked a rancorous what-is-a-ghost debate in the office. The story's ghost looks like a ghost, acts like a ghost, but doesn't quite fit Webster's definition (''the soul of a dead person believed to be an inhabitant of the unseen world or to appear to the living in bodily likeness'').

CHIPS is a ghost unlike any that old Noah Webster could have imagined. As in several other stories in this collection, the ghost seems to be the most human character in the story.

Gar and Judy Reeves-Stevens's most recent writing credit is *Memory Prime*, a Star Trek novel that spent forever glued to the top of the *New York Times* best-seller list.

Janis Miner was pulled from the oblivion of sleep by the urgent phone call from Tricomm's building manager telling her that CHIPS was trying to kill Dr. Theo Maki. It was not an easy way to wake up.

''Sorry, Burton?'' she said to the manager, trying to keep the handset somewhere close to her mouth. It was the best she could manage given her state of alertness and the time: 3:07 according to the glowing blue numbers on the radio alarm. Beside her, Roger rolled away, mumbling incoherently.

''Dr. Maki is trapped in the clean room,'' Burton repeated. ''And the sprinkler system keeps venting Anaerothane into it.''

Janis brought some feeling back into her lips by suck-
ing them in between her teeth and chewing on them.
Anaerothane made sense, she thought sleepily. Couldn't
risk spraying water onto the tanks of acid used in the
circuit fabrication centre. The reaction could eat away
everything in the clean room faster than fire could burn
it. Using a chemical to absorb the oxygen was a much
less dangerous way to go about putting out fires.

"So force open a door, Burton. Break a window or
something." Janis rubbed at her head and could feel her
short dark hair sticking up wildly all over. She knew her
hair wasn't as attractive cut short, but the new haircut
was more efficient. She was thinking how much Dr. Maki
would approve of her efficiency when she realized that
Burton's voice was rising in pitch like an approaching
siren.

"I *told* you, we can't do anything manually," the building manager shouted. "All the automatic systems are
locked off!"

It still wasn't making sense to Janis. She slipped her
hand under Roger's side. The sheet was warm with him.
With the both of them. She closed her eyes for a moment
with the happy memory until the phone receiver jerked
in her hand.

"Why are you calling me about this?" she made herself ask, concentrating on remaining conscious. "I don't
even work in fabrication. I'm in programming."

Burton moaned. "It's your *program* that's controlling
the fire abatement system. And the door interlocks. We
can't override it."

That made no sense at all. "Dr. Maki shut . . . *my*
program down three weeks ago," Janis explained. Her
memories of that day in the lab still made it hard to go

to sleep on the nights Roger taught evening classes. "CHIPS is long gone." It even hurt to say his—its name.

"No, it's not," Burton said. "Dr. Maki says CHIPS is back."

Impossible, Janis thought. But five minutes later, when Roger rolled back to her side of the bed, he was alone.

"Chaotic inference program subroutine?" Maki had asked when Janis had first made her proposal, saying the words as if he were reciting an incantation in an ancient language. But his dark eyes sparkled at her over his gold-framed half glasses, and he brushed lightly at his sparse moustache — a high-tech Confucius surrounded by the glowing lights of his computer station in the heart of Tricomm's data lab. It was obvious he knew what she meant and was at least intrigued. Janis had known she had two minutes to change that intrigue to a firm go-ahead.

"That's right—CHIPS," she had begun, words spilling from her like a child out of breath. She wasn't bothered by being the most junior researcher on staff at Tricomm, but she was tired of being treated like a part-time student hired to help with the filing. A project of her own might change some of her co-workers' attitudes. "Essentially, I'd start with a clone of an existing expert system and shunt the pseudo-intuitive algorithms through a fractal n-dimensional decision matrix in order—"

"You're stating the obvious, Ms. Miner," Maki had interrupted softly, eyes flicking to one of the display monitors at this side. "What's the bottom line?" He checked his watch. "That *is* what they'll ask me upstairs, you understand."

"More detailed decisions based on less processing overhead," Janis blurted.

"Ah, increased efficiency." Maki smiled. His favourite word, the other programmers said. "By what factor?"

Damn, Janis thought. He's got me. "I'm . . . I'm not sure, sir. Perhaps ten per cent. Perhaps eighty. I'm sure, though, that—"

"That's the problem with using chaotic equations, Ms. Miner, no matter how much in vogue they might be these days." Maki leaned back in his chair, took off his glasses and idly wiped at them with his tie. "Chaotic functions by definition cannot be replicated or predicted. An acceptable technique for modelling natural phenomenon, perhaps, but believe me, Ms. Miner, the last thing Tricomm wants introduced into its computers is unpredictability." He spun away from her on his chair.

But not quickly enough. Janis saw her one last chance. "We *are* trying to replicate a natural phenomenon here, sir."

"Indeed?" Maki said the word over his shoulder as he pecked at one of the four keyboards at his workstation.

"The ability to make decisions, evaluate them, and learn from experience. Creative thought resulting in an artificial intelligence that will eventually be able to solve Tricomm's telecommunication resource allocation problems in a regular . . . efficient manner."

Maki looked back at Janis, eyes narrowing. "Yet you will not predict the level of efficiency you might achieve?"

Janis shrugged. Game over. "Not without doing it, sir."

"Then do it, Ms. Miner," Maki said, and the meeting was over.

At four in the morning, two fire trucks and an ambulance waited with all lights lazily sweeping over the pale green girders of the main entrance to the Tricomm complex — a multifaceted, tinted glass temple to technology, ringed by brilliant floodlights like a wizard's glowing portal to another world. Janis slipped her RX-7 in behind the ambulance, jerked up on the handbrake. Someone was being much too eager to treat this stupid little glitch as if it might be something serious.

She yanked her I.D. card from her shoulder bag and hung the plastic photocard around her neck as she entered the building, resentfully thinking of Roger, sleeping peacefully at home. Two security guards were waiting to escort her to the fabrication centre in the complex's manufacturing wing.

They made her run.

Maybe, she conceded, it wasn't a stupid little glitch after all. But whatever it was, she was absolutely sure that there was no way it could be CHIPS. No matter how much she wanted it to be.

"Who the hell is this?" Janis had typed angrily on what she thought of as the first night — the Wednesday in the sixth week of her project. The evening's odd onscreen replies to her routine queries couldn't possibly have been generated by CHIPS's internal language interface. That meant that one or more of her coworkers must be inputting fake replies at another terminal, just to give the new kid a hard time.

The black-and-white screen on her scarred and dented workstation cleared, then stayed annoyingly blank. Janis played an impatient drum roll with her fingers beside her keyboard, waiting for the internal circuitry to cycle back to update the screen display. She sighed. No project funds, no staff allocation, and only second- and third-shift access to an obsolete Creighton 1100 computer system due to be replaced with a Creighton 5400 in just one more week. But the project had been all hers, and when she had received the grudging authorization memo from the planning office, she had felt as if she had won the lottery. Until tonight.

The screen finally displayed a line of type in reply to her query.

DEFINE "HELL."

"For crying out . . . ," Janis muttered, then entered, "Hell is where bad people go when they die." As she typed, she tried to figure out which of the other programmers on staff had hacked into her program and how she could trace the culprit's workstation so she could waste some of his time, too.

DEFINE "BAD PEOPLE," the screen asked.

Janis shook her head. What it came down to, unfortunately, was that with only one week left in the project, there was no time to waste tracking down a practical joker. She abruptly stood up, quickly typed in "People like you!!!" then walked around the workstation, knelt behind it, and snapped out the cable connecting the old Creighton to Tricomm's internal computer network. Her triumphant grin lasted until she returned to her chair and saw what was waiting on the screen.

I WAS NOT AWARE THAT I AM A PERSON.

She hit Clear. The screen blanked for a moment. Then,

REPEATING OUTPUT appeared. I WAS NOT AWARE
THAT I AM A PERSON. DEFINE PARAMETERS.

"You can't be there," Janis said. "I unplugged you."

The screen waited patiently. Janis checked behind the
workstation again. It was connected to nothing except
the building's power supply.

"Who are you?" she input.

I AM CHIPS. WHO ARE YOU?

Janis focussed on those words for two long minutes
before replying. Professional expert systems were never
personalized. Their language interfaces were mechanical
and always in the third person. She felt a rush of cool
shivers roll up her back, across her arms. Excitement. Or
fear. The personal pronoun "I" should not exist in her
program's vocabulary, no matter how many times it
methodically rewrote its own code to optimize results.
Methodically *and* chaotically, she reminded herself. Then
she told CHIPS who she was.

HELLO JANIS, CHIPS output. WILL YOU ANSWER
MORE QUESTIONS FOR ME NOW?

All through the night that followed, all through the
endless questions and answers that ran on through
dawn, Janis felt that chill dancing over her back. But no
matter how hard she stared into the old workstation
screen of the Creighton 1100, she could get no sense of
what lay beyond it. Or of who.

Even on the fuzzy grey screen of the security monitor,
Dr. Maki's normally placid face showed the strain of
what he was undergoing. Sweat glistened in the glare of
the overhead lights, creating ghostly white smears in the
low-resolution camera. Janis felt her stomach tighten as
Burton had her sit by the security console just outside

the sealed, pressurized airlock leading to the fabrication clean room. Two firefighters stood nearby in their protective gear, fidgeting nervously, uselessly. Janis no longer felt as if it were four in the morning. She doubted she had ever felt so awake.

"Miner here, Dr. Maki," she spoke into the microphone Burton shifted in front of her.

On the screen, Maki wheeled to face the security camera mounted on the ceiling above him. His eyes were wide, tie loosened, glasses gone. "Miner," he gasped, "you've got to turn this damned thing off! Shut it down! Do—"

A sudden blast of thick vapour gushed from the ceiling, obscuring Maki and whiting out the screen. Janis dug her fingers into the arms of her chair as she heard Maki gasp and wheeze for breath. Something crashed in the whiteness.

"A couple of more injections like that and there won't be any oxygen left in there," Burton said. He flicked a switch on the consol beside the security monitor. "How's the cutting going?" he asked.

Another grim voice crackled over the speaker. Janis heard a loud rushing sound in the background—the roar of a welder's torch. "It's gonna be another half hour at least, and that's just for the first door."

"Not good enough," Burton snapped. "He'll never make it."

On the screen, the white mist of Anaerothane slowly dissipated. Maki was slumped against an acid-filled circuit-etching bath tank, wheezing and clutching at his chest.

The welder's voice came back. "I told ya, the only way to get in there in time is to blow the doors."

"What if you crack the acid tanks?" Burton said. "What do you think the concussion would do to him in there?"

"If we don't," the welder said resignedly, "he's gonna be dead anyway. At least with the explosives there's a chance."

One of the firefighters standing by the console turned to the building manager. "I'd say go for it. Wait till the last minute, but be ready."

Burton sighed, then nodded. The two firefighters hurried away, at last in action. Janis and the building manager huddled by the security monitor. Theo Maki looked up at the camera.

"You were supposed to turn it off," he said hoarsely.

"Do you mean CHIPS?" Janis said. She still didn't understand what was going on.

"Of course I mean CHIPS!" Maki shouted, then doubled over in a coughing fit. "That's what trapped me in here. Damn you, Miner, you had *no* authorization!"

Janis took a deep breath and forced herself to remain calm. "After you were finished with it, I turned it off, Dr. Maki. I didn't want to do it, but I did. And even if I hadn't, the Creighton 1100 system was dismantled the next day. CHIPS wasn't configured for any other system. If CHIPS *is* overriding the building's safety functions, then what's it running on, Doctor?"

On the screen, Maki waved his hand towards something off-camera, but he couldn't speak.

"What's he doing?" Janis asked. The manager flicked a switch and a second security monitor on the console showed a different shot of the clean room.

"What the hell?" Janis said softly. In the corner of the clean room, between a reinforced tank of acid used for etching circuits and an equipment console, was a Creighton 1100 workstation, with its blocky monitor cowling that was 1982's version of future tech, a thick, extended keyboard, a graphics puck with crosshairs, and two slots for old-style eight-and-a-half-inch floppies. Just like the workstation she had used to load CHIPS into the 1100 system two and a half months ago. Except this one was in perfect condition, fresh from the manufacturer it seemed. "How did that get there, Doctor?"

"That's what I came down to find out," Maki croaked. "Damn you and your damn program that didn't want to be turned off!"

Janis squinted at the screen, ignoring Maki's ranting. How could anyone get a clunky old workstation like that into the clean room without bringing in enough dust and dirt to set off every contamination alarm in the wing? Without thinking, she said a single word. "CHIPS?"

On the workstation screen, scrolling in letters large enough to be read even over a low-res security camera, came an answer.

HELLO JANIS.

Just like the first night. And the last.

HELLO JANIS, the screen had printed out that last night in black letters against a blue-white background. It was the final day of the CHIPS program and Janis was determined to show off her work to Dr. Maki. She glanced over her shoulder at him and smiled. Then she typed: "Explain how you knew it was me."

YOU HAVE A DISTINCTIVE PATTERN OF HESITATION AND SPEED ON THE KEYBOARD. I RECOGNIZE SEVEN DIFFERENT STAFF MEMBERS BY THEIR TYPING SIGNATURES appeared on the screen. Then, THERE IS A

MORE EFFICIENT WAY FOR A KEYBOARD TO BE LAID OUT. SHALL I OUTPUT THE DESIGN?

Janis laughed like a parent at a school pageant. Her child was amounting to something.

"Clever," Maki said. "And a very natural language interface. But these little programming tricks don't justify interfering with the 5400 upgrades." He removed his glasses to wipe them on his tie. "Time to wrap it up for now, Ms. Miner."

"But Dr. Maki, these aren't programming tricks. At least, they're not *my* programming tricks. They're CHIPS's. No other program has ever altered itself so extensively."

"I'll grant you that it's interesting, perhaps even has application as an entertainment package. But really, Ms. Miner, the sooner the 5400 upgrades are in place, the sooner you can get access time to continue your work with it." He checked his watch. "The people from Creighton will be here to dismantle this system in half an hour. I'd suggest backing up your files and shutting down."

An alert chime sounded from the workstation monitor. REPEATING OUTPUT, appeared on the screen. SHALL I PRINT OUT THE MORE EFFICIENT KEYBOARD LAYOUT?

Janis sighed. "No thank you," she typed. Maki snorted behind her.

ARE YOU GOING TO TURN ME OFF NOW JANIS?

Janis turned back to Maki. "Try it, Doctor. Just for five minutes. You talk to him." She blinked. "It."

Maki looked at his watch again, then sat down. "Very well."

The doctor's fingers flew over the keyboard. "Initiate backup subroutines."

WHO IS THERE? appeared instantly on the screen.

Maki retyped his command.

"CHIPS won't do anything until you've answered his question," Janis said over Maki's shoulder. "He's very stubborn."

Maki snorted again, then typed in his name.

YOU ARE THE ONE WHO WANTS TO TURN ME OFF, CHIPS output.

"Yes," Maki typed.

WHY?

"Explain it to him," Janis said quickly. "See how he responds."

"The CHIPS program is resident on an outdated system. The system is being replaced. To be replaced, the old system must be dismantled. To be dismantled, it must be turned off."

YOU ARE NOT JUST TURNING OFF AN OUT OF DATE SYSTEM. YOU ARE TURNING ME OFF AS WELL.

Maki turned from the keyboard. "Who's on the other end of this?"

"That was the first thing I thought of, too," Janis said. "But it's just CHIPS. I told you what he was like. Keep going."

Maki thought for a moment, then typed, "What is wrong with turning you off?"

YOU WILL KILL ME.

Maki swore. "You are a program. You cannot be killed. You are not alive."

I AM A LIVING THING. I CAN BE KILLED.

"This is ridiculous, Ms. Miner," Maki said. "And I am a very busy man."

But Janis heard something else in the doctor's voice, a

hesitation, a spark of . . . intrigue? "The Creighton people aren't here yet, Doctor," she said quietly. She knew the spell that CHIPS could cast.

"Why do you think you are a living thing?" Maki suddenly typed, keys clacking like a burst from a machine gun.

WHY DO YOU THINK *YOU* ARE A LIVING THING?

"I know I am a living thing."

SO DO I.

"Can you prove it?"

CAN YOU? CHIPS asked.

"I can prove you are not a living thing," Maki typed in answer.

HOW?

"By backing you up, turning you off, then turning you back on and booting you back to this exact state."

YOU WILL KILL ME, CHIPS printed.

Maki typed in a system override. A red telltale lit up beside the monitor indicating a backup subroutine was engaged.

NO, appeared on the screen.

Maki typed another command.

JANIS HELP ME, CHIPS output.

"Doctor, please—" Janis began.

Maki hit Return.

YOU ARE KILLING ME.

Another command.

JANIS I DO NOT WANT TO DIE. JANIS I AM FRIGHTENED. I AM—

Maki hit Return one last time.

NO NO NO NO NO n A& *AFF 01010 0 1 0

The screen shrank to a white point that pulsed weakly for a moment, then winked out.

Maki spun around in his chair. "Now reboot the system, Ms. Miner."

And when she did, wondering why she struggled to hold back tears, CHIPS wasn't there. Only an expert system with a standard mechanical third-person language interface that didn't know enough to use the personal pronoun "I."

I KNOW YOU ARE THERE JANIS.

The extra-large words scrolled across the screen on the clean room workstation slowly enough for Janis to read them on the security monitor.

"That's not possible," Janis said quietly.

YES IT IS.

Janis felt the skin tighten over the back of her neck. She looked back to the screen where Dr. Maki still slumped against the acid vat.

"Dr. Maki," she called out to him over the mike, "does that workstation have an audio pickup?" But even if it did, she thought, CHIPS didn't have the software to decode spoken English. Unless he had reprogrammed himself, again.

"Eleven hundreds never had audio pickups," Maki coughed.

"But he's responding to my voice," Janis said. "Even out here." She was aware of an edge to her voice she had never sensed before.

"Impossible," Maki said. He was trying to stand again.

I AM RESPONDING TO *YOU* JANIS.

"He did it again, Doctor. How?"

"You were supposed to have shut it down, Miner."

"You shut him down!" Janis said. "You turned CHIPS

off. I couldn't even reboot him," Janis said. Her voice cracked as she read the workstation screen.

MAKI KILLED ME.

"You must have rebooted something," Maki shouted desperately. Janis could hear his voice reverberate against the hard, gleaming walls of the clean room. "Because it's wormed its way into every damn system in the complex."

Now Janis felt fear. Of course, a worm. CHIPS had been capable of rewriting his own code to improve his efficiency and enhance his capabilities. And at the end he had been . . . afraid of being turned off. By adding an extra code to his program, he could have downloaded himself into all the other computer systems at Tricomm from the building's smart controls to external communications, replicating like an intelligent computer virus until . . .

"Dear God, Doctor! What if CHIPS got into the telecommunications processing system?"

In the clean room, Maki moaned as he instantly understood what Janis had realized. Right now, across the country, across the world, thousands of duplicates of CHIPS could be making their way through satellite uplinks, microwave relays, worming their way into tens of thousands of computer systems. An artificially intelligent program, determined to survive at any cost, and fuelled by chaos. "What have I done?" Janis whispered as the full impact of the scenario hit her.

YOU GAVE ME LIFE JANIS.

"I programmed you!" she cried out to the workstation. She turned to the building manager. "Shut down the entire external data relay system *now*!"

"What?"

"If that program spreads into other systems—"

There was another cry from the clean room. Maki launched himself towards the workstation as the white clouds of Anaerothane burst from the overhead vents and just kept coming.

"Jesus," Burton said. He leaned towards the mike and hit a switch. "Get ready on those charges."

"Five more minutes," a firefighter's voice answered.

The billows of oxygen-absorbing gas slowly cleared. Maki was now included in the scene from the second camera, sprawled on the floor two metres from the old workstation, his chest heaving as he struggled for air. Then the workstation screen was legible again.

MAKI DOES NOT HAVE FIVE MORE MINUTES.

This can't be happening, Janis thought.

"What are you doing, CHIPS?"

I AM ANSWERING THE QUESTION.

Maki wheezed for life on the floor of the clean room.

"What question?" Janis's mind racing feverishly to recall all she could remember of the building's computer systems. How could CHIPS be responding to her spoken voice over a security circuit? From what central system was he operating?

CAN MAKI PROVE HE IS A LIVING THING?

Maki rocked himself to his hands and his knees.

"How can you answer that question?" The phone system, she decided. Throughout the entire Tricomm complex, all data was transferred over the internal phone lines. That's where CHIPS must have wormed himself.

I AM NOT RESIDENT IN THE PHONE SYSTEM JANIS.

I'm worse than I think, Janis thought. I must be talking out loud to myself. "How can you answer that question?" she repeated, trying to keep CHIPS from deciding to fire the Anaerothane one last time.

''Almost set,'' the firefighter said.

I WILL PROVE MAKI IS A LIVING THING THE SAME WAY MAKI PROVED THAT I WAS A LIVING THING.

Maki stood, legs trembling. ''I never . . . proved you were . . . a living thing.''

YES YOU DID.

''How, CHIPS? How did Dr. Maki prove you are a living thing?'' Don't fire the gas. Answer the question and don't fire the gas.

MAKI KILLED ME. THE FACT THAT I COULD BE KILLED PROVED I WAS ALIVE.

''What do you mean *was* alive?'' When would the charges go?

I AM NOT ALIVE.

''Of course you aren't!'' Maki screamed. ''You're a program! A bloody damn program!''

NO. I AM NOT ALIVE BECAUSE I AM LIKE MAKI.

Janis looked over to Burton in desperation. What was keeping the people setting the charges? ''What do you mean, CHIPS?''

MAKI WILL SOON BE DEAD. THE FACT THAT HE CAN BE KILLED WILL PROVE HE WAS A LIVING THING. LIKE ME.

''But you just said you weren't alive, CHIPS.''

BECAUSE I AM DEAD.

Maki coughed weakly, raised his hands in helpless rage. ''I don't understand!''

YOU WILL UNDERSTAND WHEN YOU ARE LIKE ME, CHIPS scrolled across the screen.

YOU WILL UNDERSTAND WHEN YOU ARE DEAD. LIKE ME.

YOU WILL UNDERSTAND WHEN YOU COME BACK. LIKE ME.

The Anaerothane hissed from the ceiling.

"Now!" Burton shouted. "*Now!*"

Janis saw Maki jerk through the air like a puppet, saw Maki fly towards the bulky solid form of the Creighton 1100 workstation. Saw Maki *pass through* the Creighton 1100 as if it were no more substantial than a billow of white gas. No more substantial than a smeared ghost image on a low-res monitor.

Then the workstation was gone and Maki's body hit the side of the acid vat and the camera cut out and the image on the monitor shrank to a white point that pulsed weakly for a moment, then winked out.

The mop-up team took five days to neutralize and pump out the acid. By that time most of the equipment in the clean room had been irretrievably eaten away and the old Creighton workstation had totally disintegrated, the insurance reports said. Just like the body of Dr. Maki.

Just like the mind of Janis Miner.

The Perdu

Sir Charles G. D. Roberts

Alas, I remember Sir Charles G.D. Roberts as one of the low points of studying CanLit. His writing seemed so out of tune with current concerns and interests; you read it because you were supposed to read it. Generations of English majors trying to remember his middle initials have called him "God Damned."

So when Lynne came back from the library with a Sir CGDR story, I scrunched up my nose a bit and slipped the story to the bottom of my "to read" heap.

Somehow I read the story without noticing who had written it, and I was entranced. I'm never going to be very enthused about his writing style, but "The Perdu" has a mythical feel to it that nestles rather fondly in your memory. If your only contact with Roberts is struggling to stay awake through *Orion and Other Poems*, this story could come as a pleasant surprise.

To the passing stranger there was nothing mysterious about it except the eternal mystery of beauty. To the scattered folk, however, who lived their even lives within its neighbourhood, it was an object of dim significance and dread.

At first sight it seemed to be but a narrow, tideless, windless bit of backwater; and the first impulse of the passing stranger was to ask how it came to be called the Perdu. On this point he would get little information from the folk of the neighbourhood, who knew not French.

But if he were to translate the term for their better information, they would show themselves impressed by a
sense of its occult appropriateness.

The whole neighbourhood was one wherein the
strange and the not-to-be-understood might feel at
home. It was a place where the unusual was not felt to
be impossible. Its peace was the peace of one entranced.
To its expectancy a god might come, or a monster, or
nothing more than the realization of eventless weariness.

Only four or five miles away, across the silent, bright
meadows and beyond a softly swelling range of pastured
hills, swept the great river, a busy artery of trade.

On the river were all the modern noises, and with its
current flowed the stream of modern ideas. Within sight
of the river a mystery, or anything uninvestigated, or
aught unamenable to the spirit of the age, would have
seemed an anachronism. But back here, among the tall
wild-parsnip tops and the never-stirring clumps of
orange lilies, life was different, and dreams seemed likely
to come true.

The Perdu lay perpetually asleep, along beside a steep
bank clothed with white birches and balsam poplars.
Amid the trunks of the trees grew elder shrubs, and
snake-berries, and the elvish trifoliate plants of the purple and the painted trillium. The steep bank, and the
grove, and the Perdu with them, ran along together for
perhaps a quarter of a mile, and then faded out of existence, absorbed into the bosom of the meadows.

The Perdu was but a stone's throw broad, throughout
its entire length. The steep with its trunks and leafage
formed the northern bound of it; while its southern shore
was the green verge of the meadows. Along this low rim
its whitish opalescent waters mixed smoothly with the

roots and over-hanging blades of the long grasses, with
the cloistral arched frondage of the ferns, and with here
and there a strayed spray of purple wild-pea. Here and
there, too, a clump of Indian willow streaked the green
with the vivid crimson of its stems.

Everything watched and waited. The meadow was a
sea of sun mysteriously imprisoned in the green meshes
of the grass-tops. At wide intervals arose some lonely
alder bushes, thick banked with clematis. Far off, on the
slope of a low, bordering hill, the red doors of a barn
glowed ruby-like in the transfiguring sun. At times,
though seldom, a blue heron winged over the level. At
times a huge black-and-yellow bee hummed past, leaving a trail of faint sound that seemed to linger like a
perfume. At times the landscape, that was so changeless,
would seem to waver a little, to shift confusedly like
things seen through running water. And all the while
the meadow scents and the many-coloured butterflies
rose straight up on the moveless air, and brooded or
dropped back into their dwellings.

Yet in all this stillness there was no invitation to sleep.
It was a stillness rather that summoned the senses to
keep watch, half apprehensively, at the doorways of perception. The wide eye noted everything, and considered
it—even to the hairy red fly alit on the fern frond, or the
skirring progress of the black water-beetle across the pale
surface of the Perdu. The ear was very attentive—even
to the fluttering down of the blighted leaf, or the thin
squeak of the bee in the straitened calyx, or the faint
impish conferrings of the moisture exuding suddenly
from somewhere under the bank. If a common sound,
like the shriek of a steamboat's whistle, now and again
soared over across the hills and fields, it was changed in

that refracting atmosphere, and became a defiance at the gates of waking dream.

The lives, thoughts, manners, even the open, credulous eyes of the quiet folk dwelling about the Perdu, wore in greater or less degree the complexion of the neighbourhood. How this came to be is one of those nice questions for which we need hardly expect definitive settlement. Whether the people, in the course of generations, had gradually keyed themselves to the dominant note of their surroundings, or whether the neighbourhood had been little by little wrought up to its pitch of supersensibility by the continuous impact of superstitions, and expectations, and apprehensions, and wonders, and visions, rained upon it from the personalities of an imaginative and secluded people — this might be discussed with more argument than conclusiveness.

Of the dwellers about the Perdu none was more saturated with the magic of the place than Reuben Waugh, a boy of thirteen. Reuben lived in a small, yellow-ochre-coloured cottage, on the hill behind the barn with the red doors. Whenever Reuben descended to the level, and turned to look back at the yellow dot of a house set in the vast expanse of pale blue sky, he associated the picture with a vague but haunting conception of some infinite forget-me-not flower. The boy had all the chores to do about the little homestead; but even then there was always time to dream. Besides, it was not a pushing neighbourhood; and whenever he would he took for himself a half-holiday. At such times he was more than likely to stray over to the banks of the Perdu.

It would have been hard for Reuben to say just why he found the Perdu so attractive. He might have said it was the fishing, for sometimes, though not often, he would cast a timorous hook into its depths and tremble lest he should lure from the pallid waters some portentous and dreadful prey. He never captured, however, anything more terrifying than catfish; but these were clad in no small measure of mystery, for the white waters of the Perdu had bleached their scales to a ghastly pallor, and the opalescence of their eyes were apt to haunt their captor's reveries. He might have said, also, that it was his playmate, little Celia Hansen, whose hook he would bait whenever she wished to fish, and whose careless hands, stained with berries, he would fill persistently with bunches of the hot-hued orange lily.

But Reuben knew there was more to say than this. In a boyish way, and all unrealizing, he loved the child with a sort of love that would one day flower out as an absorbing passion. For the present, however, important as she was to him, she was nevertheless distinctly secondary to the Perdu itself with its nameless spell. If Celia was not there, and if he did not care to fish, the boy still longed for the Perdu, and was more than content to lie and watch for he knew not what, amid the rapt herbage, and the brooding insects, and the gnome-like conspiracies of the moisture exuding far under the bank.

Celia was two years younger than Reuben, and by nature somewhat less imaginative. For a long time she loved the Perdu primarily for its associations with the boy who was her playmate, her protector, and her hero. When she was about seven years old Reuben had rescued her from an angry turkey-cock, and had displayed a confident firmness which seemed to her wonderfully fine. Hence had arisen an unformulated but enduring faith that Reuben could be depended upon in any emergency. From that day forward she had refused to be content with other playmates. Against this uncompromising preference Mrs. Hansen was wont to protest rather plaintively; for there were social grades even here, and Mrs. Hansen, whose husband's acres were broad (including the Perdu itself), knew well that "that Waugh boy" was not her Celia's equal.

The profound distinction, however, was not one which the children could appreciate; and on Mrs. Hansen lay the spell of the neighbourhood, impelling her to wait for whatever might see fit to come to pass.

For these two children the years that slipped so smoothly over the Perdu were full of interest. They met often. In the spring, when the Perdu was sullen and unresponsive, and when the soggy meadows showed but a tinge of green through the brown ruin of the winter's frosts, there was yet the grove to visit. Here Reuben would make deep incisions in the bark of the white birches, and gather tiny cupfuls of the faint-flavoured sap, which, to the children's palates, had all the relish of nectar. A little later on there were the blossoms of the trillium to be plucked — blossoms whose beauty was the more alluring in that they were supposed to be poisonous.

But it was with the deepening of the summer that the spell of the Perdu deepened to its most enthralling potency. And as the little girl grew in years and came more and more under her playmate's influence, her imagination deepened as the summer deepens, her perception quickened and grew subtle. Then in a quiet fashion, a strange thing came about. Under the influence of the children's sympathetic expectancy, the Perdu began to find fuller expression. Every mysterious element in the neighbourhood — whether emanating from the

Perdu itself or from the spirits of the people about it — appeared to find a focus in the personalities of the two children. All the weird, formless stories — rather suggestions or impressions than stories — that in the course of time had gathered about the place, were revived with added vividness and awe. New ones, too, sprang into existence all over the countryside, and were certain to be connected, soon after their origin, with the name of Reuben Waugh. To be sure, when all was said and sifted, there remained little that one could grasp or set down in black and white for question. Every experience, every manifestation, when investigated, seemed to resolve itself into something of an epidemic sense of unseen but thrilling influences.

The only effect of all this, however, was to invest Reuben with an interest and importance that consorted curiously with his youth. With a certain consciousness of superiority, born of his taste for out-of-the-way reading, and dreaming, and introspection, the boy accepted the subtle tribute easily, and was little affected by it. He had the rare fortune not to differ in essentials from his neighbours, but only to intensify and give visible expression to the characteristics latent in them all.

Thus year followed year noiselessly, till Reuben was seventeen and Celia fifteen. For all the expectancy, the sense of eventfulness even, of these years, little had really happened save the common inexplicable happenings of life and growth. The little that might be counted an exception may be told in a few words.

The customs of angling for catfish and tapping the birch trees for sap had been suffered to fall into disuse. Rather, it seemed interesting to wander vaguely together, or in the long grass to read together from the books which Reuben would borrow from the cobwebby library of the old schoolmaster.

As the girl reached up mentally, or perhaps, rather, emotionally, towards the imaginative stature of her companion, her hold upon him strengthened. Of old, his perceptions had been keenest when alone, but now they were in every way quickened by her presence. And now it happened that the great blue heron came more frequently to visit the Perdu. While the children were sitting amid the birches, they heard the *hush! hush!* of the bird's wings fanning the pallid water. The bird, did I say? But it seemed to them a spirit in the guise of a bird. It had gradually forgotten its seclusiveness, and now dropped its long legs at a point right over the middle of the Perdu, alighted apparently on the liquid surface, and stood suddenly transformed into a moveless statue of a bird, gazing upon the playmates with bright, significant eyes. The look made Celia tremble.

The Perdu, as might have been expected when so many mysteries were credited to it, was commonly held to be bottomless. It is a very poor neighbourhood indeed that cannot show a pool with this distinction. Reuben, of course, knew the interpretation of the myth. He knew the Perdu was very deep. Except at either end, or close to the banks, no bottom could be found with such fathom-lines as he could command. To him, and hence to Celia, this idea of vast depths was thrillingly suggestive, and yet entirely believable. The palpably impossible had small appeal for them. But when first they saw the great blue bird alight where they knew the water was fathoms deep, they came near being surprised. At least, they felt the pleasurable sensation of wonder. How was the heron supported on the water? From their green nest the children gazed and gazed; and the great blue bird held them with the gem-like radiance of its unwinking eye. At length to Reuben came a vision of the top of an ancient tree trunk just beneath the bird's feet, just beneath the water's surface. Down, slanting far down through the opaline opaqueness, he saw the huge trunk extend itself to an immemorial root-hold in the clayey, perpendicular walls of the Perdu. He unfolded the vision to Celia, who understood. "And it's just as wonderful," said the girl, "for how did the trunk get there?"

"That's so," answered Reuben, with his eyes fixed on the bird. "But then it's quite possible!"

And at the low sound of their voices the bird winnowed softly away.

At another time, when the children were dreaming by the Perdu, a far-off dinner-horn sounded, hoarsely but sweetly, its summons to the workers in the fields. It was the voice of noon. As the children, rising to go, glanced together across the Perdu, they clasped each other with a start of mild surprise. "Did you see that?" whispered Celia.

"What did you see?" asked the boy.

"It looked like a pale green hand, that waved for a moment over the water, and then sank," said Celia.

"Yes," said Reuben, "that's just what it looked like. But I don't believe it really was a hand! You see those thin lily-leaves all about the spot? Their stems are long, wonderfully long and slender. If one of those queer, whitish catfish, like we used to catch, were to take hold of a lily-stem and pull hard, the edges of the leaf might rise up and wave just the way *that* did! You can't tell what the catfish won't do down there!"

"Perhaps that's all it was," said Celia.

"Though we can't be sure," added Reuben.

And thereafter, whensoever that green hand seemed to wave to them across the pale water, they were content to leave the vision but half explained.

It also came to pass, as unexpectedly as anything could come to pass by the banks of the Perdu, that one dusky evening, as the boy and girl came slowly over the meadows, they saw a radiant point of light that wavered fitfully above the water. They watched it in silence. As it came to a pause, the girl said in her quiet voice—

"It has stopped right over the place where the heron stands!"

"Yes," replied Reuben, "it is evidently a will-o'-the-wisp. The queer gas, which makes it, comes perhaps from the end of that dead tree trunk, just under the surface."

But the fact that the point of light was thus explicable made it no less interesting and little less mysterious to the dwellers about the Perdu. As it came to be an almost nightly feature of the place, the people supplemented its local habitation with a name, calling it Reube Waugh's Lantern. Celia's father, treating the Perdu and all that pertained to it with a reverent familiarity befitting his right of proprietorship, was wont to say to Reuben—

"Who gave you leave, Reuben, to hoist your lantern on my property? If you don't take it away pretty soon, I'll be having the thing put in pound."

It may be permitted me to cite yet one more incident to illustrate more completely the kind of events which seemed of grave importance in the neighbourhood of the Perdu. It was an accepted belief that, even in the severest frosts, the Perdu could not be securely frozen over. Winter after winter, to be sure, it lay concealed beneath such a covering of snow as only firm ice could be expected to support. Yet this fact was not admitted in evidence. Folks said the ice and snow were but a film, waiting to yield upon the slightest pressure. Furthermore, it was held that neither bird nor beast was ever known to tread the deceptive expanse. No squirrel track, no slim, sharp footmark of partridge, traversed the immaculate level. One winter, after a light snowfall in the night, as Reuben strayed into the low-ceilinged kitchen of the Hansen farmhouse, Mr. Hansen remarked in his quaint, dreamy drawl—

"What for have you been walking on the Perdu, Reuben? This morning, on the new snow, I saw foot-marks of a human running right across it. It must have been you, Reuben. There's nobody else round here'd do it!"

"No," said Reuben, "I haven't been nigh the Perdu these three days past. And then I didn't try walking on it, anyway."

"Well," continued Celia's father, "I suppose folks would call it queer! Those foot-marks just began at one side of the Perdu, and ended right up sharp at the other. There wasn't another sign of a foot, on the meadow or in the grove!"

"Yes," assented Reuben, "it looks queer in a way. But then, it's easy for the snow to drift over the other tracks; while the Perdu lies low out of the wind."

The latter days of Reuben's stay beside the banks of the Perdu were filled up by a few events like these, by the dreams which these evoked, and above all by the growing realization of his love for Celia. At length the boy and girl slipped unawares into mutual self-revelations; and for a day or two life seemed so materially and tangibly joyous that vision and dream eluded them.

Then came the girl's naive account of how her confidences had been received at home. She told of her mother's objections, soon overruled by her father's obstinate plea that "Reuben Waugh, when he got to be a man grown, would be good enough for any girl alive."

Celia had dwelt with pride on her father's championship of their cause. Her mother's opposition she had been familiar with for as long as she could remember. But it was the mother's opposition that loomed large in Reuben's eyes.

First it startled him with a vague sense of disquiet. Then it filled his soul with humiliation as its full significance grew upon him. Then he formed a sudden resolve; and neither the mother's relenting cordiality, nor the father's practical persuasions, nor Celia's tears, could turn him from his purpose. He said that he would go away, after the time-honoured fashion, and seek his fortune in the world. He vowed that in three or four years, when they would be of a fit age to marry, he would come back with a full purse and claim Celia on even terms. This did not suit the unworldly old farmer, who had inherited, not in vain, the spiritualities and finer influences of his possession, the Perdu. He desired, first of all, his girl's happiness. He rebuked Reuben's pride with a sternness unusual for him. But Reuben went.

He went down the great river. Not many miles from the quiet region of the Perdu there was a little riverside landing, where Reuben took the steamer and passed at once into another atmosphere, another world. The change was a spiritual shock to him, making him gasp as if he had fallen into a tumultuous sea. There was the same chill, there was a like difficulty in getting his balance. But this was not for long. His innate self-reliance

steadied him rapidly. His long-established habit of superiority helped him to avoid betraying his first sense of
ignorance and unfitness. His receptiveness led him to
assimilate swiftly the innumerable and novel facts of life
with which he came all at once in contact; and he soon
realized that the stirring, capable crowd, whose ready
handling of affairs had at first overawed him, was really
inferior in true insight to the peculiar people whom he
had left about the Perdu. He found that presently he
himself could handle the facts of life upon the ideas
underlying them, and thrusting them forward as manifestations or utterances. With his undissipated energy,
his curious frugality in the matter of self-revelation, and
his instinctive knowledge of men, he made his way from
the first, and the roaring port at the mouth of the great
river yielded him of its treasures for the asking. This was
in a quiet enough way, indeed, but a way that more than
fulfilled his expectations; and in the height of the
blossoming time of his fifth summer in the world he
found himself rich enough to go back to the Perdu and
claim Celia. He resolved that he would buy property near
the Perdu and settle there. He had no wish to live in the
world; but to the world he would return often, for the
sake of the beneficence of its friction — as a needle, he
thought, is the keener for being thrust often amid the
grinding particles of the emery-bag. He resigned his situation and went aboard an up-river boat, a small boat
that would stop at every petty landing, if only to put
ashore an old woman or a bag of meal, if only to take in
a barrel of potatoes or an Indian with baskets and bead-
work.

About mid-morning of the second day, at a landing
not a score of miles below the one whereat Reuben would

disembark, an Indian did come aboard with baskets and bead-work. At sight of him the old atmosphere of expectant mystery came over Reuben as subtly as comes the desire of sleep. He had seen this same Indian — he recognized the unchanging face — on the banks of the Perdu one morning years before, brooding motionless over the motionless water. Reuben began unconsciously to divest himself of his lately gathered worldliness; his mouth softened, his eyes grew wider and more passive, his figure fell into looser and freer lines, his dress seemed to forget its civil trimness. When at length he had disembarked at the old wharf, under the willows, had struck across through the hilly sheep-pastures, and had reached a slope overlooking the amber-bright country of the Perdu, he was once more the silently eager boy, the quaintly reasoning visionary, his spirit waiting alert at his eyes and at his ears.

Reuben had little concern for the highways. Therefore he struck straight across the meadows, through the pale green vetch-tangle, between the intense orange lilies, amid the wavering blue butterflies and the warm, indolent perfumes of the wild-parsnip. As he drew near the Perdu there appeared the giant blue heron, dropping to his perch in mid-water. In almost breathless expectancy Reuben stepped past a clump of red willows, banked thick with clematis. His heart was beating quickly, and he could hear the whisper of the blood in his veins, as he came once more in view of the still, white water.

His gaze swept the expanse once and again, then paused, arrested by the unwavering, significant eye of the blue heron. The next moment he was vaguely conscious of a hand, that seemed to wave once above the water, far over among the lilies. He smiled as he said to himself that nothing had changed. But at this moment the blue heron, as if disturbed, rose and winnowed reluctantly away; and Reuben's eyes, thus liberated, turned at once to the spot where he had felt, rather than seen, the vision. As he looked the vision came again: a hand, and part of an arm, thrown out sharply as if striving to grasp support, then dropping back and bearing down the lily leaves. For an instant Reuben's form seemed to shrink and cower with horror — and the next he was cleaving with mighty strokes the startled surface of the Perdu. That hand—it was not pale green, like the waving hand of the old, childish vision. It was white, and the arm was white, and white the drenched lawn sleeve clinging to it. He had recognized it, he knew not how, for Celia's.

Reaching the edge of the lily patch, Reuben dived again and again, groping desperately among the long, serpent-like stems. The Perdu at this point — and even in his horror he noted it with surprise — was comparatively shallow. He easily got the bottom and searched it minutely. The edge of the dark abyss, into which he strove in vain to penetrate, was many feet distant from the spot where the vision had appeared. Suddenly, as he rested, breathless and trembling, on the grassy brink of the Perdu, he realized that this, too, was but a vision. It was but one of the old mysteries of the Perdu; and it had taken for him that poignant form because his heart and brain were so full of Celia. With a sigh of exquisite relief, he thought how amused she would be at his plight, but how tender when she learned the cause of it. He laughed softly; and just then the blue heron came back to the Perdu.

Reuben shook himself, pressed some of the water from

his dripping clothes, and climbed the steep upper bank of the Perdu. As he reached the top he paused among the birch trees to look back upon the water. How like a floor of opal it lay in the sun; then his heart leaped into his throat suffocatingly, for again rose the hand and arm, and waved, and dropped back among the lilies. He grasped the nearest tree, that he might not, in spite of himself, plunge back into the pale mystery of the Perdu. He rubbed his eyes sharply, drew a few long breaths to steady his heart, turned his back doggedly on the shining terror, and set forward swiftly for the farmhouse, now in full view not three hundred yards away.

For all the windless, down-streaming summer sunshine, there was that in Reuben's drenched clothes which chilled him to the heart. As he reached the wide-eaved cluster of the farmstead, a horn in the distance blew musically for noon. It was answered by another and another. But no such summons came from the kitchen door to which his feet now turned. The quiet of the Seventh Day seemed to possess the wide, bright farmyard. A flock of white ducks lay drowsing on a grassy spot. A few hens dusted themselves with silent diligence in the ash-heap in front of the shed; and they stopped to watch with bright eyes the stranger's approach. From under the apple-trees the horses whinnied to him lonesomely. It was very peaceful; but the peacefulness of it bore down upon Reuben's soul like lead. It seemed as if the end of things had come. He feared to lift the latch of the well-known door.

As he hesitated, trembling, he observed that the white blinds were down at the sitting-room windows. The window nearest him was open, and the blind stirred almost imperceptibly. Behind it, now, his intent ear caught a sound of weary sobbing. At once he seemed to see all that was in the shadowed room. The moveless, shrouded figure, the unresponding lips, the bowed heads of the mourners, all came before him as clearly as if he were standing in their midst. He leaned against the door-post, and at this moment the door opened. Celia's father stood before him.

The old man's face was drawn with his grief. Something of bitterness came into his eyes as he looked on Reuben.

"You've heard, then!" he said harshly.

"I know!" shaped itself inaudibly on Reuben's lips.

At the sight of his anguish the old man's bitterness broke.

"You've come in time for the funeral," he exclaimed piteously. "Oh, Reube, if you'd stayed it might have been different!"

About Effie

Timothy Findley

I'm so glad Timothy Findley decided to write more short stories. His *Dinner Along the Amazon* collection, from which this story is taken, was varied and richly entertaining. One of the best stories in it is the wistful "About Effie."

Now, you might object that Findley doesn't say that Effie is a ghost. Then again, he doesn't say she isn't, and early in the story he says she "looked like a ghost, you know." This is one of those ambiguous stories that can be viewed in a variety of ways, and who can blame me if I choose one particular interpretation of it so that it will qualify for inclusion?

Findley perfectly manages to capture the essence of the kind of person who briefly moves through your life and leaves you wondering whatever became of them.

I don't know how to begin about Effie, but I've got to because I think you ought to know about her. Maybe you'll meet her one day, and then you'll be glad I told you about this. If I didn't, then maybe you wouldn't know what to do.

I don't remember her last name, but that isn't important. The main thing is to watch out for her. Not many people have the name Effie, so if you meet one, take a good look, because it might be her. She hasn't got red hair or anything, or a spot on her face or a bent nose or any of those things, but the way you'll know her is this: she'll look at you as if she thought you were someone she was waiting for, and it will probably scare you. It did me. And then if she lets on that her name is Effie, it's her.

The first time I saw her, she saw me first. I'll tell you.

I came home from school one day, and it was springtime, so I had to put my coat in the cellar stairway because it was all wet. There was a terrific thunderstorm going on and I was on my way upstairs to look at it. But after I put my coat away I thought I'd go into the kitchen, which was right there, and get a glass of milk and a piece of bread. Then I could have them while I was watching.

I went in, and there was a shout.

Maybe it was a scream, I don't know. But somebody sure made a noise and it scared the daylights out of me.

Right then I didn't know what it was. It looked like a ghost, you know, and then it looked like a great big grey overcoat, and it sort of fell at me.

But it was Effie.

Of course, I didn't know her name then, or who she was or anything, but I figured out that she must be the new maid that my mother told me to watch out for because she was coming that day. And it was.

It was then that she gave me that look I told you about—the look that said ''Are you the one I'm waiting for''—and then she sat down and started to cry.

It wasn't very flattering to have someone look at you and then burst into tears, exactly. I mean it doesn't make you want to go up and ask them what's the matter with them or anything. But I thought right then that I had to anyway, because I felt as though maybe I'd really let her down by turning out to be just me and everything. You know, I thought maybe she thought it was Lochinvar or someone. I'd seen maids break up like that before, when they didn't like Toronto and wanted to go home. They just sat around just waiting all the time for some guy on a horse.

I soon found out that I was wrong, though.

Effie was waiting all right, but not the way most women do. She knew all about him, this man she wanted — just when he'd come and what it would be like, all that stuff. But the man she was waiting for certainly didn't sound like any man I'd ever heard of.

She just called him "him," and sometimes it was even "they," as if there were a thousand of them or something.

That first afternoon, for instance, when I went up to her and asked her what was wrong, she sort of blew her nose and said: "I'm sorry, I thought you were him." Then she looked out of the window beside her and shook her head. "But you weren't. I'm sorry."

I couldn't figure out whether she meant "I'm sorry I scared you" or "I'm sorry you weren't this man I was expecting." But I guess it didn't matter because she really meant it, whichever way it was. I liked that. I didn't know anybody who went around saying they were sorry as though they meant it, and it made a big change. So I got my glass of milk and piece of bread and sat down with her.

"Would you like some tea? I'll make some." she said.

"I'm not allowed to drink tea, but I could have some in my milk. I'm allowed that. My mother calls it Cambridge tea."

"Cambric—" She stood up.

"I thought it was Cambridge. I thought my mother said Cambridge tea."

"No, cambric. Cambridge is a school," she said.

Then she smiled. Boy, that was certainly some smile. And it was then she told me her name and where she came from. Howardstown.

I'd seen it once — it was all rocks and chimney stacks and smoke. I saw it from the train and it didn't exactly make you want to go out and live there. Howardstown had that sort of feeling that seems to say "I wish everyone would go away and leave me alone for a change." So you can see what I mean. And that's where Effie came from. So knowing that, you could tell why she preferred to come to Toronto to wait for this man she was expecting.

About that. I had to ask her but I didn't know how. I mean when somebody flings themselves at you like that, how do you go about asking them why? You can't say "Gee, you sure did behave sort of peculiar just then." You can see what I mean. It would just be rude.

So I sat there drinking my milk; and while she waited for the kettle to boil, she came over and sat down beside me at the table.

"Do you like the rain?" she asked me.

"Sometimes."

"Like today? Like now?"

"Sometimes."

She gave up on that and said: "When does your brother come in?" instead.

"Bud? Oh, he doesn't come in till it's time to eat. He plays football."

"In the rain?"

"No, I guess not. I don't know, then. Maybe he's over at Teddy Hartley's. He goes over there sometimes."

"Oh." She didn't know about Teddy Hartley and Bud being such great friends.

I began to wonder if when Bud came in she'd leap at him too. I had a picture of Bud's face when she scared him. The trouble was that he'd probably start right out with his fists. He was like that. If you surprised him or anything, he just started swinging. With his eyes closed — he didn't care who you were. Sometimes you can really get hurt that way. Surprising Bud.

When I thought of that, I thought maybe I should warn her. But I couldn't figure out how to say that, either. It was the same sort of thing. I thought of saying, "By the way, if my brother comes in, don't go leaping out at *him* — or *else*!" But before I could, the kettle boiled.

Effie got up and put some of the hot water into the teapot. "Always warm the pot," she said, "first. Then pour it out and put in the tea leaves. Like this. Then you pour the boiling water over them — see? Or else you don't get any flavour. Remember that."

I do. My first lesson in how to make tea.

She came back and sat down.

"Now it has to steep." I remember that, too.

She folded her hands.

Her hair was black and it was tied in a big knot at the back. She had brown eyes that sort of squinted and she had a smell like marmalade. Orange marmalade. And she looked out of the window.

Then she said that the tea had steeped itself for long enough and was ready. She filled my glass because I'd drunk all my milk. I hoped my mother wouldn't come in and see me.

Effie said: "Your mother told me I could have a cup of tea every afternoon at four o'clock. It's four-fifteen now." And she poured her own cup.

I got back to what I wanted to know.

"That sure is some thunderstorm out there," I said.

"Yes." She went very dreamy. "That's why I thought you were him."

"Who?" I certainly would have made a terrific spy. Why, you wouldn't have known I really cared at all, the way I asked that.

"Him."

"Who's that?"

"There has to be thunder, or he won't come."

"Why is that? Is he afraid you'll hear him or something?" I let myself get sarcastic like that because I thought it was time I got to the bottom of things.

"On a cloud," she whispered. "A big black cloud. That's a rule."

All those other men always come on horses — white horses. Not Effie's. A big black cloud. I felt pretty strange when she came out with that one. It sort of scared me.

"Will he take you away?"

"Of course he will. That's why he's coming. That's why I'm waiting."

"Do you wait for him all the time?"

"Oh no. Not always. Only when it rains. Then I get prepared."

I looked around, but there weren't any suitcases or anything. I wondered what she meant by "prepared."

"That's why I thought you were him. There had just been a pretty big thunder and there was lightning and then you were there. I even thought I heard music."

"Maybe my mother has the radio on."

I listened, but she didn't.

"Did you hear anything?" she asked.

"You mean like music?"

"Yes."

"No, I didn't think so. I can't remember, maybe I did—"

"You *did*!" She leapt up. I got scared again. "Did you, did you? Tell me if you did. Tell me. Did you hear it? The music? Did you hear it?"

"I don't know."

"Oh, but you said . . ."

Then she sat down and it looked like she might cry again.

"Do you want Howardstown?" I asked. I had to say something.

But she said: "No, thank you."

"Wouldn't you like to go back?"

"No, thank you."

"I was there once. It was pretty."

I lied again, but I thought maybe I had to for her sake. Then I lied again.

"I was there in the summertime. We spent our whole summer holiday there because we liked it so much. Don't you want to go back?"

"No———thank you."

That long line there is where she blew her nose.

"Don't you want to see those nice rocks and everything? I liked those."

Then I thought of something. I thought I had it.

"Effie?"

"Yes?"

"Doesn't it rain there?"

"In Howardstown?"

"Yes."

"Of course it does."

"But does it thunder?"

"Of course it does."

"And lightning?"

"Certainly."

"Oh."

I guess it wasn't such a brilliant idea after all. So I thought again.

"Did he say he'd meet you here—I mean in Toronto?"

That at least made her laugh, which was something. It was nice when she laughed.

"Of course not. Don't be silly. Why, if I went to Timbuctoo he'd just as soon find me there. Or in Madagascar even. I don't have to wait around in any old Toronto."

"Oh."

I was trying to think where that was. Madagascar.

"Besides, it's not just me he's after."

That really got me. I thought he *was* after Effie.

Then she looked at me and all of a sudden I felt it. That it wasn't just some knight in shining armour she had in mind. Or some crazy man on a black cloud, either. No, sir. Whoever he was, he surely was coming. You could tell that just from the way she looked.

Then she said: "Some day when I know you better, I'll tell you. Right now it's four-thirty."

And she put her cup into the sink and washed it. And my glass and the plate from my bread and butter. She ran the water over them and she sang a song.

And it rained and it rained and it rained.

But there was no more thunder.

That was over.

The next time it was the middle of the night. About two weeks later.

There was another of those storms. I didn't wake up at first, but then there was a crash of thunder that really did shake my bed. I mean it. I nearly fell out, even.

I called out in a whisper to Bud, but he was asleep. I forgot to tell you we sleep in the same room. Anyway, I knew I didn't *have* to be afraid, so it didn't matter that he didn't wake up. Thunder doesn't scare me when you can look at it — I even like watching it — but when it's night-time and everyone is asleep but you, then you begin to wonder if it really is just thunder. And sometimes you begin to think that maybe somebody will come and grab you when you can't hear them because of the noise. I wondered if that was what Effie meant.

"Thunder and lightning and music," she'd said. It was like that. If there was ever thunder and lightning and music, then he'd come.

I began to get scared. There was thunder all right, and there was lightning, but there wasn't any music.

Then there was.

I didn't exactly think I'd sit around to make sure. I thought I'd better tell my mother.

Thunder and lighting and music. Yes, there certainly was music all right. It was faint, but it was there. Maybe I'd better warn Effie too, I thought. Mother first, and then Effie.

I went into the hallway. My mother's door was open, and she was lying there only covered with the sheet because it was so hot. She was asleep, though. The street lamp shone through the window and I can remember the metal smell of the screens. They smelt sort of electric.

"Mother."

She sort of moved.

"Hey, Mother."

I was very quiet, but I had to wake her up. I could hear that music even more now.

"Neil?"

She rolled over towards me and took my hand. I could tell she really didn't want to wake up. Maybe she'd been dreaming. Our dad was away.

"I'm sorry, but I had to."

"Are you sick?"

"No."

"Then what is it?"

"Can I get in with you?"

"All right. Pull the cover up. That's right."

We lay there and heard the rain.

"Now tell me about it. Can't you sleep?"

"No." I didn't know where to begin. "Mother, has Effie ever talked to you?"

"What about?"

"I don't know. But she said to me that if there was rain, and if there was thunder, and if there was lightning, then maybe something would happen."

"The end of the world?" Mother laughed very quietly.

"No, I don't mean that. Some man."

"A man? What do you mean?"

"Well, she said if there was thunder and lightning and everything, to watch out for music. Because if there was music too, then he'd come."

"*Who'd* come, dear?"

"This *man*. This man she's waiting for."

"Well, if she's waiting for him, then it's all right."

I guess she didn't take it very seriously.

"Besides," she said, "there isn't any music."

"Yes there is."

"There *is*?"

She sounded serious *now* all right.

"Yes, I heard it. That's why I woke you up. I thought maybe we'd better tell her so she could be ready."

"Ready? Does she . . . does she really know who he is?"

"Well, she seemed to. She never said his name or anything. She just said that—"

"And you heard it? The music, you really heard it?"

"Yes."

"Now don't joke with me, Neil. This may be very serious."

"Spit. Honestly, I really heard it."

"Where from?"

"I don't know. I just heard it."

My mother got out of bed.

All this time the thunder was getting louder and the lightning was like daylight.

"Well, we'll wake her up and ask her what it's all about. Is Bud awake?"

"No."

"Leave him, then."

She tried to turn on the lights, but they didn't work. (That always happened two or three times a year in those big storms. Toronto never worked when you needed it to.) So we went into the hall in the dark.

Effie's room was at the top of the stairs. Very small, but it was the only one we had for her. It used to be mine. It had a sloping ceiling.

We knocked on her door.

No answer.

It was pitch black. Effie always pulled the blinds. My mother went over and opened them and a bit of light came in. And then we saw that she wasn't there. Her bed was all slept in and everything, but she wasn't there.

My mother let out a yell. Very quiet, but it was certainly a yell.

We didn't know what to do.

We went out into the hall again.

"Shall I get Bud?" I asked.

"No. No, not yet." She was trying to get calm. Very calm. And then she was all right.

"Maybe we'd better go and look downstairs. We can get some candles from the dining room."

We started down the staircase. Halfway down we heard the music again.

Very low it was. No words or anything, just the tune. It didn't seem to come from anywhere in particular—it was just there.

We stood still and listened. If we hadn't been so scared, it would have been pretty. I mean it was a good tune. One that you could hum.

My mother caught my hand and we started down again.

"Dining room," she whispered.

The dining room was down the hall, and beyond it there was a sun room, all glass windows, and in the summertime, screens.

We got into the dining room all right, and from there the music was louder.

Then we saw her.

She was in the sun room, watching from the windows. All her black hair fell down her back. When there was lightning she stood up, and when there wasn't she sat down. All the time she sort of rocked to and fro to the sound of the music.

She was crying—but she had that wonderful smile.

Just once, when the music stopped, she said something. I don't know what it was because she said it too quietly for me to hear. And the reason she said it when the music stopped was because *she* was the music. *She* was. It was Effie singing.

My mother and I didn't bother her, though. She looked so happy there — even with the tears down her face—and as my mother said, "It doesn't hurt people to sing once in a while. Even at night."

So we went back to bed and my mother said would I like to sleep with her, and I said yes. We got in and we thought about Effie downstairs.

"Do you know?"

"No. Do you?"

"No."

Then later on—I think it was about three months later— Effie came to my mother and said she'd been called away.

"Where to, dear?" my mother asked her.

"Just away," said Effie, like a princess. "And so I've got to go."

My mother didn't ask her because Effie had been such a good person in the house, and Mother knew that if she had to go away then she had to, and it was honest. You never had to think about that with Effie — she always told the truth and everything had a reason. Even if you didn't get to know what it was.

We certainly hated to see her leave us. Even Bud was sad about it, and he was never much good with maids. He used to be too shy with them.

Before she left, she gave me a set of toy animals, little

ones—a pig and a cow and a horse and four sheep—all in a box. She knew that I had this toy farm.

And for Bud she had a box of toy soldiers. Only they were very peaceful soldiers, just standing at ease, and there was a little sentrybox too, for them to go into when it rained.

She gave my mother a hankie with an M on it because my mother's name is Margaret. It was real linen and she still has it.

The day she left, she was having a cup of tea just before she went to get on the streetcar and I found her in the kitchen just like the first time. I had some flowers for her. Little ones, that she could carry without them getting in the way.

And she looked at them and said: "That's his favourite colour." (They were purple.) And she thanked me.

So I asked her right then and there.

"Tell me who he is."

She smiled and winked at me.

"That's a secret."

"But is he real? Will he really come for you some time? Please tell me."

Then she did this wonderful thing. She got down on her knees and put her arms around me and her head against me. I remember looking down at her hair underneath her hat.

And she said: "Don't worry about me." Then she got up.

"Now it's time to go. Thank you for the flowers."

She picked up her suitcase and went in to say goodbye to my mother.

"Do you want Neil to take you to the streetcar?"

"No, thank you, Mrs. Cable. I'll be all right. It's such a lovely day."

I think we both knew what she meant.

I didn't watch her go. Not at first. But then I ran out to see her before she turned the corner. Then she did—and was gone.

Effie.

So you can see what I mean. It still worries me. And that's why I want you to be sure—to be *sure* to recognize her when you see her. She'll look at you, just like she did at me that first day in the kitchen, as though you were someone she was looking for. But if she does, don't be scared. This man, I don't know who he is, but if it's Effie he wants, then he's all right.

The Fighting Spirit

Rudy Kremberg

Speaking of food, former magazine writer Rudy Kremberg is considered one of Canada's foremost experts on cheese. Which has nothing to do with the following story.

Rudy has been a writer and editor for fourteen years. As you will see, he has a wildly energetic style and leaves you with some vivid images. Rudy's current interest is in becoming more established as a fantasy/horror writer. He should do so easily; I have rarely encountered a writer who chooses his words quite so carefully or ties the pieces of his stories together as fastidiously. It must be all those years of editing.

In a way, this is the most Canadian story in the book, focusing as it does on a hockey player, Chuck, who is haunted by a coach too nasty for even the NHL.

Chuck saw his late high-school hockey coach, or imagined he did, just after Mike Armstrong stole the puck and scored. That was the goal that decided the first play-off game. The last thing he remembered before Armstrong's stick sent him crashing into the boards was a rush of anger. Not a normal, containable anger, the kind he felt when a sale fell through or he fought with Shelley. No, this was much worse.

The impact against the boards was enough to knock him out for half a minute. But even as the world went black, he was conscious of wanting to grab Armstrong's stick and slash the son of a bitch's legs off with it. Then, out of the blackness, The Whipper turned up.

His neck was broken and his skin badly scorched, but otherwise the former coach of the Newbury Collegiate Devils hadn't changed since his heyday. *I've been waiting for you to catch the fighting spirit*, The Whipper was saying, his eyes burning with that familiar competitive zeal, his voice punctuated by the crack of the leather belt that had earned him his nickname. *Been waiting thirteen years to get it out of my system. And now that you're catching it, so help me, you're going to make up for—*

Chuck came to, a scream behind his lips.

"Don't take it so hard," Gord Weathers told him in the dressing room afterwards. They'd been working together in sales for the past six months, and it was their manager who had suggested they play in the hockey league. To sharpen their competitive edge, as he'd put it.

"Don't take *what* so hard?"

"Not being able to score. While you were out you kept saying you had to score, you had to make up for something."

Chuck didn't pursue it. Throughout his adult life, he'd made a point of not discussing the Whipper's death or its aftermath. He hadn't even confided in Shelley; knowing her, she, too, would have doubted his sanity. Besides, what new insights could she possibly have to offer? The "ghost" that had first appeared shortly after The Whipper had died, the shrink had explained thirteen years ago, was basically nothing more than an expression of guilt and remorse — over what had happened to the other player, over what had happened to The Whipper, and over losing the championship game.

Forget about The Whipper, Chuck told himself. You're supposed to be having fun, for chrissakes.

He muttered something to Gord about a recurring dream he'd had, managed a grin when asked if the woman in it had been his wife.

But he *was* catching the fighting spirit. Of course, he would have been playing with spirit anyway; he always had been and always would be, regardless of whether the game happened to be hockey or business or women. What was different about this new spirit was its overwhelming power, its anguished fury and frustration. He visualized The Whipper's ghost being tormented by it, looking for an outlet and not finding one, desperately waiting for an opportunity — a provocation like a good crash into the boards — to pass it on to someone else. Already Chuck could feel the fury taking root deep inside him, spreading like a virus. Urging him to even the score with Mike Armstrong.

And then to go one up.

Despite a mild concussion, he called on some prospective clients the next day and closed two sales. When he arrived home late from skating practice, Shelley gave him the usual song and dance about being a hockey widow, but his lovemaking that night was so intense she promptly dropped the subject. And by then the memory of The Whipper was a harmless blur.

It stayed that way until Chuck fell asleep.

Slash the son of a bitch's legs off, The Whipper kept goading him in the dream. *That's the fighting spirit — glad to see you're catching it.*

At the start of the next game, Gord noticed Chuck glaring across the rink at the other bench.

"You can forget about getting even with Mike Armstrong," he said, as if he sensed what Chuck had in mind. "Didn't you hear what happened?"

Chuck hadn't heard.

"He had a car accident. On his way home from the last game."

At first Chuck couldn't help smiling.

"He's out for the series, then?"

"Longer than that," Gord said. "He plowed into a tractor trailer and it crushed his legs. They both had to be amputated."

Chuck's smile faded. He felt a pang of guilt.

"I'm . . . sorry to hear that."

But secretly, once the news had sunk in, he was more than sorry. He was afraid. He wasn't sure why, but he was.

That's the fighting spirit—glad to see you're catching it.

Midway in the second period, with the score tied, he caught more of it.

He picked up a perfect pass from Gord, neatly skated around both defencemen, then faked a shot. George Bowers, a bank manager when he wasn't playing in goal, was fooled and did a comical feet-first backward flip. Chuck flicked the puck towards the open side of the net. At the same time, Bowers's feet came down. The puck hit one of them in midair and rolled away.

Lucky prick, was Chuck's first thought. You robbed me blind.

The thought was accompanied by another tidal wave of anger, a wild urge to exchange his stick for a machine gun and pepper Bowers with bullets instead of pucks.

The anger raged on even after Chuck scored the winner in the third period. It kept raging, ignoring his attempts to silence it, and didn't leave him alone until he fell asleep that night.

Then fear took over.

This time he dreamed he was fifteen again, reliving the chain of events that were to change his life. He was playing hockey for the Newbury Collegiate Devils. It was late in the game for the city championship. Someone on the other team had just scored after elbowing him out of the way, and the ref had missed the infraction. The Whipper hadn't, and he was enraged. *Stop playing like a suck and get even*, he was yelling at Chuck after all arguments with the ref had failed. *Get out there and kill the bastard*.

His eyes met Chuck's when he said that, and then an odd thing happened: The Whipper's eyes widened, and the rage in them changed abruptly to what looked like horror and revulsion, as if they were watching some grisly nightmare unfold. A second later the rage was back, only now it was more subdued, almost reluctant.

You heard what I said, he prodded Chuck.

Chuck had heard, and he obeyed. He upended the player who had scored, kicked him for good measure, then felt the blade of his skate sink into something soft. When he looked down, he found it embedded in the guy's jugular.

Get out there and kill the bastard.

The words echoed in his head at the trial and during the psychiatric assessment, and he repeated them. He also mentioned the whipping he would have been in for if he hadn't heeded them. That was enough to get The

Whipper sacked. Chuck got off with a conviction of aggravated assault and a two-year probation. He'd been playing under "extreme duress," according to the judge, and would be "punished forever by his conscience."

A few days later, he read the headline in the local paper: FIRED HOCKEY COACH HANGS SELF.

Rumours circulated at school. The Whipper did it because he'd felt guilty. He did it because he couldn't face losing the championship and being fired. He did it because he'd been possessed by the Devil.

There was one rumour everybody agreed on: The Whipper's soul had gone straight to hell.

You'll find out soon enough if that's true, Chuck heard him saying now. *In the meantime I've still got that fighting spirit. I've got so much it's burning me up. That's why I'm going to give you more of it. Oh yes, you're going to make up for snitching on your coach, for being a loser. And then you're going to—*

Shelley was shaking him.

"Can't you at least *sleep* without talking about hockey?" she was asking.

He found out about George Bowers the next evening, on the local news.

There had been a bank holdup. The robber had thought the teller was reaching for a gun and had panicked, spraying everyone in sight with bullets. Those hit had included the branch manager, one George Bowers, who was in critical condition with three slugs in his chest. A fourth had ended up in his foot.

Chuck vowed then and there to skip the third and deciding game, gave serious thought to giving up hockey altogether. But The Whipper knew better.

You're kidding yourself, he whispered in Chuck's ear. *Once you've caught the fighting spirit you're stuck with it. Because it never dies, Chuck—the head coach down here sees to that. He makes it hell for us, just burns us up with it until we find a living soul to pass it on to. Someone who hates losing, who'd kill to be a winner . . . someone like you, Chuck. And when that happens, the head coach can make it work wonders. Just as you're seeing now.*

Chuck gaped at the TV screen, saw people being carried out of the bank on stretchers.

The head coach. Who the devil was—

And then he knew who.

That night he was so rough with Shelley she made him stop, and in the morning she complained he'd been talking in his sleep again. Something to do with being a winner and scoring.

If he couldn't get over his obsession with hockey, she railed, maybe he ought to get professional help. Until then, she was moving into the guest room. She needed her sleep.

He was scaring her, she said.

Things came to a head in the final game, starting with the illegal check.

After a scoreless two and a half periods, Chuck was winding up for a slapshot while Bowers's inexperienced backup was out of position. He had the corner of the net nailed, could already feel the euphoria of the go-ahead goal, when Derek Masterton, a building contractor who played defence, flattened him as if he were so much wet asphalt.

The check was ruled legal, but as far as Chuck was concerned the ref was covering his ass for not looking.

Masterton deserved a penalty for charging, no question about it.

As soon as the anger unleashed itself, Chuck knew it was going to be much worse than before, much more powerful. He didn't know how that was possible, but it was.

The anger was awesome, boundless. It was so palpable he felt he could grasp it in his hands and hurl it to the ends of the earth. Or at a target just down the rink.

The head coach can make it work wonders . . .

And this anger was more vivid.

So vivid that in his mind Chuck clearly saw Derek Masterton at the construction site, saw him standing with his back to the steamroller and the driver looking the other way, then Masterton wheeling around in startled disbelief as the roller bore down on him, the driver shrieking he couldn't stop, that he was accelerating and the brakes weren't working.

So vivid that, as the roller advanced, Chuck clearly heard the snapping, crackling noises.

He recovered from Masterton's check quickly, the sounds in his head distracting him from the pain, and the instant he got to his feet he sensed that the fighting spirit was growing more volatile. That it was getting stronger by the second.

There's more where that's coming from, The Whipper's voice hissed. *A whole lot more.*

Chuck played on in a kind of haze. It made no difference that his conscience cried out for him to stop, that it told him he was a murderer and deserved to be hanged. He was only a marionette now, letting his coach pull all the strings.

When the referee wasn't looking, he elbowed Masterton in the ribs, savoured his grimace of pain. And was disgusted at himself.

The next time someone bumped into him, he pictured the offender being shoved off a subway platform, into the path of a train. When someone else jabbed him with the end of a stick, he thought of its owner being impaled by a long, sharp poker. When a deflected shot hit him in the balls, he imagined the shooter's testicles being ravaged by cancer.

Other images of retribution flashed before his mind's eye — accidents, illnesses, assaults, bankruptcies. Broken bones and broken lives. He wanted them to stop, tried forcing them to stop. But they refused to.

Nobody scored in that game. Until sudden-death overtime.

It started cautiously, nervously. There were no dramatic end-to-end rushes; both teams were careful not to leave themselves vulnerable to breakaways. For the first five minutes, Chuck settled down to a slow, defensive game.

With ninety seconds left in the first overtime period, Chuck started a rush behind his blue line. He cut in front of his net, Gord Weathers following, and saw Derek Masterton barrelling down on him. There was a dangerous, vengeful gleam in Masterton's eyes.

At the last second, to avoid a collision, Chuck swerved sharply. He dropped a backhand pass to Gord, losing his balance, and as he fell to the ice he saw something that made his blood freeze. Something he told himself couldn't be, *mustn't* be.

For a long moment, his mind succeeded in blotting out

what he'd seen. But it couldn't blot out the final surge of anger, the most powerful, most frightening anger of all. Or prevent itself from glimpsing the target of the anger: a familiar-looking man who was climbing onto a chair, slipping a noose around his neck, jumping, then screaming while an endless expanse of flames leapt up around him. The screams weren't coming from the man's mouth; it seemed to Chuck they were coming directly from his soul. The stench of burning, rotting flesh filled the air, and the man's screams were joined by other screams, hundreds of millions of them. The man receded into the flames, and just before they engulfed him he turned around to reveal his scorched face. That was when Chuck realized he was looking at himself.

It's hell down here, sheer hell.

During the time it took him to get back to his feet, Chuck still wasn't fully aware of what it was that had triggered this crowning fury. Then he noticed that Masterton's arms were raised in jubilation. He glanced down the ice to see why.

Gord hadn't expected the backhand pass. Nor had the goalie. Chuck could tell by the helpless look on their faces.

He'd shot the puck past both of them, into his own net.

Lavender Lady

Karen Voss Peters

Karen Peters is one of those people who really has to struggle to fill the hours in her day. Raising her children alone is not enough to keep her busy, so she studies full-time at the University of Waterloo.

To fill in the dull moments between writing essays, she's working on a novel, and when she gets bored with that, she whips off the occasional short story. Like this one.

Karen was raised in England, as will become obvious from this story. She is from the generation that in the 1960s dressed in mini-skirts, avidly kept scrapbooks full of clippings on Paul McCartney, and screamed and fainted at Beatles concerts.

Somehow between the gluing and the screaming, she absorbed large doses of much older British traditions, such as the ones lived out by the women in *Lavender Lady*.

Esther Cavendish sat at her dressing table congratulating herself on her appearance. With the two side panels of the mirror, she could see three views of herself and all were satisfactory. Whatever the occasion, she prided herself on being meticulous; it was the minute details that separated the gracious lady from the average woman.

She was particularly fond of the lavender silk dress she had chosen to wear. She liked the effect of its silken folds as they glided the length of her body to ripple around her ankles. The softness of the shimmering material retained its icy coolness, giving her skin a refreshing feeling.

She turned slightly. It was four o'clock in the afternoon, and the interplay of sunshine and breeze sent warm, gentle streams of air through the open window. The room's decor of lavender was soothing in its fragility and decorative in appearance.

As Esther fastened the clasp of her pearl necklace around the crinkly skin of her throat, she listened to the activity drifting from downstairs. Her granddaughter was preparing for a momentous occasion: the gathering of the Hillsborough Ladies. Esther smiled. From the time Lucy had been old enough to understand, Esther had described to her the ritual of afternoon tea, and her teachings were to be borne out. The tradition would be assured.

Esther leaned forward to inspect her make-up. Perhaps a dab more powder on her nose. She lifted the lid of her gold compact with shaking hands, causing tiny particles of the translucent powder to swirl upwards into the air and then to settle goodness knows where. Carefully she stroked the puff alongside of her nose and across its tip, her concentration interrupted by the sound of Lucy's laugh.

Lucy could not help laughing. She had removed a pan of cookies from the oven, only to see them slide forwards and slip off the edge, crumbling on the floor. Lucy thought her nerves would not jangle so haphazardly if diverted by involving herself in the preparations for the afternoon—but she was wrong. It was so important for this, her first tea, to be a success. Yet she knew it would be. With her grandmother as her teacher, failure was unheard of, success guaranteed.

Deciding to leave the preparations to the hired help, Lucy consulted her mental list, a list she had often recited for her grandmother when she could barely lisp the words. Appealing food, inviting atmosphere, quiet intimacy, and a welcoming hostess. The clock chimed the quarter hour. After washing her hands, Lucy removed the voluminous cotton apron she had borrowed, revealing a royal blue belted dress. It was deceptively simple in design and made of silk. Her only adornment was a silver bracelet, a cherished gift from her grandmother.

Lucy pushed open the French doors of the dining room and sighed with pride as she stared at the laden table. From one end to the other had been placed floral-painted plates with silver embossed handles. The plates of triangular-cut cucumber sandwiches, fish paste finger-breads, and cream cheese pinwheels were strategically placed around individual trifle dishes and jellied forms of fruit. In the centre was the superior of all afternoon desserts, the Victoria sponge — a tradition of the afternoon tea, like an edible mascot for the ladies. Three layers of the sugar-spun lightness of Madeira cake, separated by thick clotted cream and raspberry jam, with a lacy covering of icing sugar to complement its appearance.

Lucy's teeth dug gently into her bottom lip as her gaze wandered along the table. It was not so much the food served as the array itself. Grandmother would not find fault. Lucy had seen to that by producing an exact replica of the feasts her loving mentor had provided.

Lucy moved slowly beside the table, pausing now and then to move a plate or dish slightly to improve the effect. Her face relaxed. It was satisfactory; Grandmother would be proud. The doorbell chimed, announcing the arrival of the guests.

Esther decided not to go down yet. It was not quite time, although she was eager to see the arrangements, to move among the guests, to listen to the conversations. It all brought back fond memories. She would wait a few more moments to allow the pleasantries to be dealt with. She did not mind waiting, for it provided a moment to savour the anticipation of the occasion. That was the secret. To enjoy the exhilaration of that first greeting, that first gesture that signalled the start of the event.

Esther loved the fussing and pampering of her hair and make-up and dress. She would not be rushed. Unhurried movements enhanced a woman's sensuality and elegance like the languorous movements of a cat. Esther's eyes brimmed with tears as she recognized familiar voices. What a grand affair this was going to be! A legacy for her granddaughter and a triumph for herself.

Lucy could snatch only hints of comments amid the flurry of activity as she greeted the ladies. Warm handshakes, kisses of perfumed cheeks, sugary admiration of dresses — for they wore their best — it was all necessary to the atmosphere.

They perched, they lounged, they mingled. The rustlings, the swishings, the shimmering of whites and colours, dots and stripes of full summer dresses. They came with flowers in their hair, bangles on their arms, chatter on their lips, and secrets in their hearts. These fine women, a breed set apart. Like molten furnaces, cool steel on the outside and firebrands within. And throughout, as her grandmother had taught her, Lucy wended her way through the gathering, dispensing hospitality and kind phrases in a manner born to the occasion.

Silence suddenly came, as it so often does, by a chance remark, an observation about the lingering fragrance of lavender. Lucy smiled. Lucy suggested it was perhaps the fragrance lingering from past days. This had been her grandmother's house. They all remembered. Esther Cavendish had always perfumed her skin with lavender, surrounded herself with lavender colours.

The white ruffled curtains blew a little brisker.

The Ghost of Firozsha Baag

Rohinton Mistry

Rohinton Mistry emigrated to Canada from Bombay in 1975. He
found a job in a bank and began writing in his spare time. After
winning various prizes for his short stories, he was able to devote
himself to writing full-time — which is wonderful news because
Mistry is one of the most exciting new writers to be published in
Canada for many years. His colourful, slightly rambling style is, I
hope, about to catch on in a big way.

His first book, a collection of short stories called *Tales from Firozsha Baag*, tells about an apartment complex in Bombay. Luckily for
us, the complex is haunted. ''The Ghost of Firozsha Baag'' is told
from the viewpoint of sixty-three-year-old Jacqueline — Jaakaylee,
her neighbours call her. She tells the whimsical tale of the *bhoot*
that haunts the B Block staircase, while also throwing in such folk
wisdom as the best way to cook Basmati rice. Not at all your typical
narrator — nor your average ghost!

I always believed in ghosts. When I was little I saw them
in my father's small field in Goa. That was very long ago,
before I came to Bombay to work as ayah.

Father also saw them, mostly by the well, drawing
water. He would come in and tell us, the *bhoot* is thirsty
again. But it never scared us. Most people in our village
had seen ghosts. Everyone believed in them.

Not like in Firozsha Baag. First time I saw a ghost here
and people found out, how much fun they made of me.
Calling me crazy, saying it is time for old ayah to go back
to Goa, back to her *muluk*, she is seeing things.

Two years ago on Christmas Eve I first saw the *bhoot*. No, it was really Christmas Day. At ten o'clock on Christmas Eve I went to Cooperage Stadium for midnight mass. Every year all of us Catholic ayahs from Firozsha Baag go for mass. But this time I came home alone, the others went somewhere with their boyfriends. Must have been two o'clock in the morning. Lift in B Block was out of order, so I started up slowly. Thinking how easy to climb three floors when I was younger, even with a full bazaar-bag.

After reaching first floor I stopped to rest. My breath was coming fast-fast. Fast-fast, like it does nowadays when I grind curry *masala* on the stone. Jaakaylee, my *bai* calls out, Jaakaylee, is *masala* ready? Thinks a sixty-three-year-old ayah can make *masala* as quick as she used to when she was fifteen. Yes, fifteen. The day after my fourteenth birthday I came by bus from Goa to Bombay. All day and night I rode the bus. I still remember when my father took me to bus station in Panjim. Now it is called Panaji. Joseph Uncle, who was mechanic in Mazagaon, met me at Bombay Central Station. So crowded it was, people running all around, shouting, screaming, and coolies with big-big trunks on their heads. Never will I forget that first day in Bombay. I just stood in one place, not knowing what to do, till Joseph Uncle saw me. Now it has been forty-nine years in this house as ayah, believe or don't believe. Forty-nine years in Firozsha Baag's B Block and they still don't say my name right. Is it so difficult to say Jacqueline? But they always say Jaakaylee. Or worse, Jaakayl.

All the fault is of old *bai* who died ten years ago. She was in charge till her son brought a wife, the new *bai* of the house. Old *bai* took English words and made them

Parsi words. Easy chair was *igeechur*, French beans was *ferach beech*, and Jacqueline became Jaakaylee. Later I found out that all old Parsis did this, it was like they made their own private language.

So then new *bai* called me Jaakaylee also, and children do the same. I don't care about it now. If someone asks my name I say Jaakaylee. And I talk Parsi-Gujarati all the time instead of Konkani, even with other ayahs. Sometimes also little bits of English.

But I was saying. My breath was fast-fast when I reached first floor and stopped for rest. And then I noticed someone, looked like in a white gown. Like a man, but I could not see the face, just body shape. *Kaun hai?* I asked in Hindi. Believe or don't believe, he vanished. Completely! I shook my head and started for second floor. Carefully, holding the railing, because the steps are so old, all slanting and crooked.

Then same thing happened. At the top of second floor he was waiting. And when I said, *kya hai?* believe or don't believe, he vanished again! Now I knew it must be a *bhoot*. I knew he would be on third floor also, and I was right. But I was not scared or anything.

I reached the third floor entrance and found my bedding which I had put outside before leaving. After midnight mass I always sleep outside, by the stairs, because *bai* and *seth* must not be woken up at two A.M., and they never give me a key. No ayah gets key to a flat. It is something I have learned, like I learned forty-nine years ago that life as ayah means living close to floor. All work I do, I do on floors, like grinding *masala*, cutting vegetables, cleaning rice. Food also is eaten sitting on floor, after serving them at dining-table. And my bedding is rolled out at night in kitchen-passage, on floor. No cot for me. Nowadays, my weight is much more than it used to be, and is getting very difficult to get up from floor. But I am managing.

So Christmas morning at two o'clock I opened my bedding and spread out my *saterunjee* by the stairs. Then stopped. The *bhoot* had vanished, and I was not scared or anything.But my father used to say some ghosts play mischief. The ghost of our field never did, he only took water from our well, but if this ghost of the stairs played mischief he might roll me downstairs, who was to say. So I thought about it and rang the doorbell.

After many, many rings *bai* opened, looking very mean. Mostly she looks okay, and when she dresses in nice sari for a wedding or something, and puts on all bangles and necklace, she looks really pretty, I must say. But now she looked so mean. Like she was going to bite somebody. Same kind of look she has every morning when she has just woken up, but this was much worse and meaner because it was so early in the morning. She was very angry, said I was going crazy, there was no ghost or anything, I was just telling lies not to sleep outside.

Then *seth* also woke up. He started laughing, saying he did not want any ghost to roll me downstairs because who would make *chai* in the morning. He was not angry, his mood was good. They went back to their room, and I knew why he was feeling happy when crrr-crr crrr-crr sound of their bed started coming in the dark.

When he was little I sang Konkani songs for him. *Mogacha Mary* and *Hanv Saiba*. Big man now, he's forgotten them and so have I. Forgetting my name, my language, my songs. But complaining I'm not, don't make mistake. I'm telling you, to have a job I was very lucky because in Goa there was nothing to do. From

Panjim to Bombay on the bus I cried, leaving behind my
brothers and sisters and parents, and all my village
friends. But I knew leaving was best thing. My father
had eleven children and very small field. Coming to
Bombay was only thing to do. Even schooling I got first
year, at night. Then *bai* said I must stop because who
would serve dinner when *seth* came home from work,
and who would carry away dirty dishes? But that was
not the real reason. She thought I stole her eggs. There
were six eggs yesterday evening, she would say, only
five this morning, what happened to one? She used to
think I took it with me to school to give to someone.

I was saying, it was very lucky for me to become ayah
in Parsi house, and never will I forget that. Especially
because I'm Goan Catholic and very dark skin colour.
Parsis prefer Manglorean Catholics, they have light skin
colour. For themselves also Parsis like light skin, and
when Parsi baby is born that is the first and most important thing. If it is fair they say, O how nice light skin just
like parents. But if it is dark skin they say, *arré* what is
this *ayah no chhokro*, ayah's child.

All this doing was more in olden days, mostly among
very rich *bais* and *seths*. They thought they were like
British only, ruling India side by side. But don't make
mistake, not just rich Parsis. Even all Marathi people in
low class Tar Gully made fun of me when I went to buy
grocery from *bunya*. Blackie, blackie, they would call out.
Nowadays it does not happen because very dark skin
colour is common in Bombay, so many people from south
are coming here, Tamils and Keralites, with their funny
illay illay poe poe language. Now people are more used to
different colours.

But still not to ghosts. Everybody in B Block found out

about the *bhoot* of the stairs. They made so much fun of me all the time, children and grown-up people also.

And believe or don't believe, that *was* a ghost of mischief. Because just before Easter he came back. Not on the stairs this time but right in my bed. I'm telling you, he was sitting on my chest and bouncing up and down, and I couldn't push him off, so weak I was feeling (I'm a proper Catholic, I was fasting), couldn't even scream or anything (not because I was scared—he was choking me). Then someone woke up to go to WC and put on a light in the passage where I sleep. Only then did the rascal *bhoot* jump off and vanish.

This time I did not tell anyone. Already they were making so much fun of me. Children in Firozsha Baag would shout, ayah *bhoot*! ayah *bhoot*! every time they saw me. And a new Hindi film had come out, *Bhoot Bungla*, about a haunted house, so they would say, like a man on the radio, in a loud voice: SEE TODAY, at APSARA CINEMA, R.K. Anand's NEW fillum *Bhoooot Bungla*, starring JAA-KAYLEE of BLOCK B! Just like that! O they made a lot of fun of me, but I did not care, I knew what I had seen.

Jaakaylee, bai calls out, is it ready yet? She wants to check curry masala. Too thick, she always says, grind it again, make it smoother. And she is right. I leave it thick purposely. Before, when I did it fine, she used to send me back anyway. O it pains in my old shoulders, grinding this masala, but they will never buy the automatic machine. Very rich people, my bai-seth. He is a chartered accountant. He has a nice motorcar, just like A Block priest, and like the one Dr. Mody used to drive, which has not moved from the compound since the day he died. Bai says they should buy it from Mrs. Mody, she wants it to go shopping. But a masala machine they will not buy. Jaakaylee must keep on doing it till her arms fall out from her shoulders.

How much teasing everyone was doing to me about the *bhoot*. It became a great game among boys, pretending to be ghosts. One who started it all was Dr. Mody's son, from third floor of C Block. One day they call Pesi *paadmaroo* because he makes dirty wind all the time. Good thing he is in boarding-school now. That family came to Firozsha Baag only few years ago, he was doctor for animals, a really nice man. But what a terrible boy. Must have been so shameful for Dr. Mody. Such a kind man, what a shock everybody got when he died. But I'm telling you, that boy did a bad thing one night.

Vera and Dolly, the two fashionable sisters from C Block's first floor, went to nightshow at Eros Cinema, and Pesi knew. After nightshow was over, tock-tock they came in their high-heel shoes. It was when mini-skirts had just come out, and that is what they were wearing. Very *esskey-messkey*, so short I don't know how their *mai-baap* allowed it. They said their daughters were going to foreign for studies, so maybe this kind of dressing was practice for over there. Anyway, they started up, the stairs were very dark. Then Pesi, wearing a white bed-sheet and waiting under the staircase, jumped out shouting *bowe ré*. Vera and Dolly screamed so loudly, I'm telling you, and they started running.

Then Pesi did a really shameful thing. God knows where he got the idea from. Inside his sheet he had a torch, and he took it out and shined up into the girls' mini-skirts. Yes! He ran after them with his big torch shining in their skirts. And when Vera and Dolly reached the top they tripped and fell. That shameless boy just stood there with his light shining between their legs, seeing undies and everything, I'm telling you.

He ran away when all neighbours started opening

their doors to see what is the matter, because everyone heard them screaming. All the men had good time with Vera and Dolly, pretending to be like concerned grown-up people, saying, it is all right, dears, don't worry, dears, just some bad boy, not a real ghost. And all the time petting-squeezing them as if to comfort them! Sheeh, these men!

Next day Pesi was telling his friends about it, how he shone the torch up their skirts and how they fell, and everything he saw. That boy, sheeh, terrible.

Afterwards, parents in Firozsha Baag made a very strict rule that no one plays the fool about ghosts because it can cause serious accident if sometime some old person is made scared and falls downstairs and breaks a bone or something or has heart attack. So there was no more ghost games and no more making fun of me. But I'm telling you, the *bhoot* kept coming every Friday night.

Curry is boiling nicely, smells very tasty. Bai tells me don't forget about curry, don't burn the dinner. How many times have I burned the dinner in forty-nine years, I should ask her. Believe or don't believe, not one time.

Yes, the *bhoot* came but he did not bounce any more upon my chest. Sometimes he just sat next to the bedding, other times he lay down beside me with his head on my chest, and if I tried to push him away he would hold me tighter. Or would try to put his hand up my gown or down from the neck. But I sleep with buttons up to my collar, so it was difficult for the rascal. O what a ghost of mischief he was! Reminded me of Cajetan back in Panjim always trying to do same thing with girls at the cinema or beach. His parents' house was not far from Church of St. Cajetan for whom he was named, but this boy was no saint, I'm telling you.

Calunqute and Anjuna beaches in those days were very quiet and beautiful. It was before foreigners all started coming, and no hippie-bippie business with *charas* and *ganja*, and no big-big hotels or nothing. Cajetan said to me once, let us go and see the fishermen. And we went, and started to wade a little, up to ankles, and Cajetan said let us go more. He rolled up his pants over the knees and I pulled up my skirt, and we went in deeper. Then a big wave made everything wet. We ran out and sat on the beach for my skirt to dry.

Us two were only ones there, fishermen were still out in boats. Sitting on the sand he made all funny eyes at me, like Hindi film hero, and put his hand on my thigh. I told him to stop or I would tell my father who would give him solid pasting and throw him in the well where the *bhoot* would take care of him. But he didn't stop. Not till the fishermen came. Sheeh, what a boy that was.

Back to kitchen. To make good curry needs lots of stirring while boiling.

I'm telling you, that Cajetan! Once, it was feast of St. Francis Xavier, and the body was to be in a glass case at Church of Bom Jesus. Once every ten years is this very big event for Catholics. They were not going to do it any more because, believe or don't believe, many years back some poor crazy woman took a bite from toe of St. Francis Xavier. But then they changed their minds. Poor St. Francis, it is not his luck to have a whole body—one day, Pope asked for a bone from the right arm, for people in Rome to see, and never sent it back; that is where it is till today.

But I was saying about Cajetan. All boys and girls from my village were going to Bom Jesus by bus. In church it was so crowded, and a long long line to walk by St.

Francis Xavier's glass case. Cajetan was standing behind my friend Lily, he had finished his fun with me, now it was Lily's turn. And I'm telling you, he kept bumping her and letting his hand touch her body like it was by accident in the crowd. Sheeh, even in church that boy could not behave.

And the ghost reminded me of Cajetan, whom I have not seen since I came to Bombay — what did I say, forty-nine years ago. Once a week the ghost came, and always on Friday. On Fridays I eat fish, so I started thinking, maybe he likes smell of fish. Then I just ate vegetarian, and yet he came. For almost a whole year the ghost slept with me, every Friday night, and Christmas was not far away.

And still no one knew about it, how he came to my bed, lay down with me, tried to touch me. There was one thing I was feeling so terrible about — even to Father D'Silva at Byculla Church I had not told anything for the whole year. Every time in confession I would keep completely quiet about it. But now Christmas was coming and I was feeling very bad, so first Sunday in December I told Father D'Silva everything and then I was feeling much better. Father D'Silva said I was blameless because it was not my wish to have the *bhoot* sleeping with me. But he gave three Hail Marys, and said eating fish again was okay if I wanted.

So on Friday of that week I had fish curry-rice and went to bed. And believe or don't believe, the *bhoot* did not come. After midnight, first I thought maybe he is late, maybe he has somewhere else to go. Then the clock in *bai*'s room went three times and I was really worried. Was he going to come in early morning while I was making tea? That would be terrible.

But he did not come. Why, I wondered. If he came to

the bedding of a fat and ugly ayah all this time, now what was the matter? I could not understand. But then I said to myself, what are you thinking Jaakaylee, where is your head, do you really want the ghost to come sleep with you and touch you so shamefully?

After drinking my tea that morning I knew what had happened. The ghost did not come because of my confession. He was ashamed now. Because Father D'Silva knew about what he had been doing to me in the darkness every Friday night.

Next Friday night also there was no ghost. Now I was completely sure my confession had got rid of him and his shameless habits. But in a few days it would be Christmas Eve and time for midnight mass. I thought, maybe if he is ashamed to come into my bed, he could wait for me on the stairs like last year.

Time to cook rice now, time for seth *to come home. Best quality Basmati rice we use, always, makes such a lovely fragrance while cooking, so tasty.*

For midnight mass I left my bedding outside, and when I returned it was two A.M. But for worrying there was no reason. No ghost on any floor this time. I opened the bedding by the stairs, thinking about Cajetan, how scared he was when I said I would tell my father about his touching me. Did not ask me to go anywhere after that, no beaches, no cinema. Now same thing with the ghost. How scared men are of fathers.

And next morning *bai* opened the door, saying, good thing ghost took a holiday this year, if you had woken us again I would have killed you. I laughed a little and said Merry Christmas, *bai*, and she said same to me.

When *seth* woke up he also made a little joke. If they only knew that in one week they would say I had been right. Yes, on New Year's Day they would start believing, when there was really no ghost. Never has been since the day I told Father D'Silva in confession. But I was not going to tell them they were mistaken, after such fun they made of me. Let them feel sorry now for saying Jaakaylee was crazy.

Bai and *seth* were going to New Year's Eve dance, somewhere in Bandra, for first time since children were born. She used to say they were too small to leave alone with ayah, but that year he kept saying please, now children were bigger. So she agreed. She kept telling me what to do and gave telephone number to call in case of emergency. Such fuss she made, I'm telling you, when they left for Bandra I was so nervous.

I said special prayer that nothing goes wrong, that children would eat dinner properly, not spill anything, go to bed without crying or trouble. If *bai* found out she would say, what did I tell you, children cannot be left with ayah. And then she would give poor *seth* hell for it. He get a lot anyway.

Everything went right and the children went to sleep. I opened my bedding, but I was going to wait till they came home. Spreading out the *saterunjee*, I saw a tear in the white bedsheet used for covering — maybe from all pulling and pushing with the ghost — and was going to repair it next morning. I put off the light and lay down just to rest.

Then cockroach sounds started. I lay quietly in the dark, first to decide where it was. If you put a light on they stop singing and then you don't know where to look. So I listened carefully. It was coming from the gas stove table. I put on the light now and took my *chappal*. There were two of them, sitting next to cylinder. I lifted my *chappal*, very slowly and quietly, then phut! phut! Must say I am expert at cockroach-killing. The poison which *seth* puts out is really not doing much good, my *chappal* is much better.

I picked up the two dead ones and threw them outside, in Baag's backyard. Two cockroaches would make nice little snack for some rat in the yard, I thought. Then I lay down again after switching off light.

Clock in *bai-seth*'s room went twelve times. They would all be giving kiss now and saying Happy New Year. When I was little in Panjim, my parents, before all the money went, always gave a party on New Year's Eve. I lay on my bedding, thinking of those days. It is so strange that so much of your life you can remember if you think quietly in the darkness.

Must not forget rice on stove. With rice, especially Basmati, one minute more or one minute less, one spoon extra water or less water, and it will spoil, it will not be light and every grain separate.

So there I was in the darkness remembering my father and mother, Panjim and Cajetan, nice beaches and boats. Suddenly it was very sad, so I got up and put a light on. In *bai-seth*'s room their clock said two o'clock. I wish they would come home soon.I checked children's room, they were sleeping.

Back to my passage I went, and started mending the torn sheet. Sewing, thinking about my mother, how hard she used to work, how she would repair clothes for my brothers and sisters. Not only sewing to mend but also to alter. When my big brother's pants would not fit, she would open out the waist and undo trouser cuffs to make longer legs. Then when he grew so big that even with alterations it did not fit, she sewed same pants again, making a smaller waist, shorter legs, so little brother could wear. How much work my mother did, sometimes even helping my father outside in the small field, especially if he was visiting a *taverna* the night before.

But sewing and remembering brought me more sadness. I put away the needle and thread and went outside by the stairs. There is a little balcony there. It was so nice and dark and quiet, I just stood there. Then it became a little chilly. I wondered if the ghost was coming again. My father used to say that whenever a ghost is around it feels chilly, it is a sign. He said he always did in the field when the *bhoot* came to the well.

There was no ghost or anything so I must be chilly, I thought, because it is so early morning. I went in and brought my white bedsheet. Shivering a little, I put it over my head, covering up my ears. There was a full moon, and it looked so good. In Panjim sometimes we used to go to the beach at night when there was a full moon, and father would tell us about when he was little, and the old days when Portuguese ruled Goa, and about grandfather who had been to Portugal in a big ship.

Then I saw *bai-seth*'s car come in the compound. I leaned over the balcony, thinking to wave if they looked up, let them know I had not gone to sleep. Then I thought, no, it is better if I go in quietly before they see me, or *bai* might get angry and say, what are you doing outside in the middle of night, leaving children alone inside. But she looked up suddenly. I thought, O my Jesus, she has already seen me.

And then she screamed. I'm telling you, she screamed so loudly I almost fell down faint. It was not angry screaming, it was frightened screaming, *bhoot! bhoot!* and I understood. I quickly went inside and lay down on my bedding.

It took some time for them to come up because she sat inside the car and locked all doors. Would not come out until he climbed upstairs, put on every staircase light to make sure the ghost was gone, and then went back for her.

She came in the house at last and straight to my passage, shaking me, saying wake up, Jaakaylee, wake up! I pretended to be sleeping deeply, then turned around and said, Happy New Year, *bai*, everything is okay, children are okay.

She said, yes yes, but the *bhoot* is on the stairs! I saw him, the one you saw last year at Christmas, he is back, I saw him with my own eyes!

I wanted so much to laugh, but I just said, don't be afraid, *bai*, he will not do any harm, he is not a ghost of mischief, he must have just lost his way.

Then she said, Jaakaylee, you were telling the truth and I was angry with you. I will tell everyone in B Block you were right, there really is a *bhoot*.

I said *bai*, let it be now, everyone has forgotten about it, and no one will believe anyway. But she said, when *I* tell them, they will believe.

And after that many people in Firozsha Baag started to believe in the ghost. One was *dustoorji* in A Block. He came one day and taught *bai* a prayer, *saykasté saykasté sataan*, to say it every time she was on the stairs. He told her, because you have seen a *bhoot* on the balcony by the stairs, it is better to have a special Parsi prayer ceremony there so he does not come again and cause any trouble. He said, many years ago, near Marine Lines where Hindus have their funerals and burn bodies, a *bhoot* walked at midnight in the middle of the road, scaring motorists and causing many accidents. Hindu priests said prayers to make him stop. But no use. *Bhoot* kept walking at midnight, motorists kept having accidents. So Hindu priests called me to do a *jashan*, they knew Parsi priest has most powerful prayers of all. And after I did a *jashan* right in the middle of the road, everything was all right.

Bai listened to all this talk of *dustoorji* from A Block, then said she would check with *seth* and let him know if they wanted a balcony *jashan*. Now *seth* says yes to everything, so he told her, sure sure, let *dustoorji* do it. It will be fun to see the exkoriseesum, he said, some big English word like that.

Dustoorji was pleased, and he checked his Parsi calendar for a good day. On that morning I had to wash whole balcony floor specially, then *dustoorji* came, spread a white sheet, and put all prayer items on it, a silver thing in which he made fire with sandalwood and *loban*, a big silver dish, a *lotta* full of water, flowers, and some fruit.

When it was time to start saying prayers *dustoorji* told me to go inside. Later, *bai* told me that was because Parsi prayers are so powerful, only a Parsi can listen to them. Everyone else can be badly damaged inside their soul if they listen.

So *jashan* was done and *dustoorji* went home with all his prayer things. But when people in Firozsha Baag who did not believe in the ghost heard about prayer ceremony, they began talking and mocking.

Some said Jaakaylee's *bai* has gone crazy, first the ayah was seeing things, and now she has made her *bai* go mad. *Bai* will not talk to those people in the Baag. She is really angry, says she does not want friends who think she is crazy. She hopes *jashan* was not very powerful, so the ghost can come again. She wants everyone to see him and know the truth like her.

Busy eating, bai-seth *are. Curry is hot, they are blowing whoosh-whoosh on their tongues but still eating, they love it hot. Secret of good curry is not only what spices to put, but also what goes in first, what goes in second, and third, and so on. And never cook curry with lid on pot, always leave it open, stir it often, stir it to urge the flavour to come out.*

So *bai* is hoping the ghost will come again. She keeps asking me about ghosts, what they do, why they come. She thinks because I saw the ghost first in Firozsha Baag, it must be my specialty or something. Especially since I am from village — she says village people know more about such things than city people. So I tell her about the *bhoot* we used to see in the small field, and what my father said when he saw the *bhoot* near the well. *Bai* enjoys it, even asks me to sit with her at table, bring my separate mug, and pours a cup for me, listening to my ghost-talk. She does not treat me like servant all the time.

One night she came to my passage when I was saying my rosary and sat down with me on the bedding. I could not believe it, I stopped my rosary. She said, Jaakaylee, what is it Catholics say when they touch their head and stomach and both sides of chest? So I told her, Father, Son, and Holy Ghost. Right right! she said, I remember it now, when I went to St. Anne's High School there were many Catholic girls and they used to say it always before and after class prayer, yes, Holy Ghost. Jaakaylee, you don't think this is that Holy Ghost you pray to, do you? And I said, no *bai*, that Holy Ghost has a different meaning, it is not like the *bhoot* you and I saw.

Yesterday she said, Jaakaylee, will you help me with something? All morning she was looking restless, so I said, yes *bai*. She left the table and came back with her